Heindt
The End of Yesterdays

1

MANSFRED SWRIT

ISBN-13: 978-0-9986390-1-7
978-0-9986390-7-9 (eBook)

First Edition

1 2 3 4 5 6 7 8 9 10

Heindt
The End of Yesterdays

1

1

The gentle breeze flittered across the open fields of barely-tamed grass as it made its way up and through the bright, green leaves of the field's lone tree. The sunlight seemed to sparkle as the leaves jostled in protest at the disturbance. Thick streams of light made their way through the canopy and into the shade below, bringing their brilliance to the only hint of darkness in the bright, beautiful landscape.

The comforting warmth of the sun gave just the right touch of perfection to the idyllic surrounding. And the steady *thunk* of dull-metal beating on wood gave the perfect rhythm to the blissful day.

Elliana's eyes shot open as she felt her head loll to one side. It was then that she realized how dangerously close she was to toppling over side of the low stone wall. If her torso had leaned forward just a little more, her unintended nap would have had a significantly less pleasant ending.

She took a deep breath, inhaling the clean, fresh air, which quickly turned into a deep yawn. She rubbed her blurry eyes, which slowly turned into a deep stretch of almost all of her muscles.

Her stone-wall seat was located just behind her home on the very edge of town. This allowed a picturesque view of the surrounding landscape. From the wall, the land sloped gently until it eventually flattened into a large meadow where a lone but proud tree stood tall and sturdy, taking its duty as sentinel seriously. Littered around the tree were several wooden pells and other equipment, collectively called the 'training ground'.

But, to Elliana, it was a stage.

Each movement of the performer provided a note and a step, and each note and step flowed into a song and dance. The instrument of choice for the day's environmental score was a hefty-looking training sword with a dull-metal edge. Despite its size, the performer played his instrument with such elegance and finesse that even a seasoned veteran might have mistaken the sword's heft. However, the loud ring of metal striking wood would challenge that conclusion.

Elliana shook her head in an attempt to rid the stubborn bits of sleep that clung to her senses. She wasn't very successful.

It was only natural for her to fall asleep to the hypnotic beat as the gentle, late-morning warmth lulled her with comfort. The sight of the elegant dance with its exciting flourishes should have been more than enough to raise the heart rate despite the calming ambiance. But the comfort and routine, and possibly fatigue, were just too difficult to beat.

Elliana sighed. She rested her head in her palms, and rested her elbows on her thighs. She was determined to pay attention, though she really had no reason to.

And as her senses slowly woke and sharpened, she suddenly felt the chill of a cold, dark shadow behind her. Her heart rate was not lulled any longer. She quickly spun her head in an attempt to ward off the cold presence, but she was too late.

A hand covered Elliana's mouth and roughly pulled her back behind the low wall. She yelped and flailed her limbs, but her yelp was muffled and her flailing limbs were soon brought under control. Her arms were pinned on the ground by a forceful hand while another covered her mouth. Elliana was determined to not give in without a fight. All she had to do was to get free long enough to get someone's attention.

Elliana kicked her legs as hard as she could in all directions. She arched her back off the ground as far as she could. With the momentum of her kicks, she was able to get her back high off the ground and almost to the point where she could feel freedom.

But somehow a third hand grabbed one of her legs, fingers gripping into the fleshiness of her thigh, and pinned it down. Chills went down Elliana's arched spine which gave pause to her struggle. It was more than enough for a fourth hand to grab a hold of her other leg. It didn't stop there: the shadowy figure proceeded to mount her and pin her with their weight.

Elliana's pulse quickened and so did her thoughts. Unfortunately, she could not think of a way out. All she could think about was 'why this happening in such a safe town?' and 'why it had to be her of all people?'.

The attacker loomed over her, their weight fully pressing her into the hard dirt path. Elliana dared herself to meet the shadow's eyes, but the bright sun overhead obscured her vision and made the shadow's features hard to see. But before she closed her eyes again, she swore she had seen a hint of a sinister smile.

The sound of movement above her head caught her unaware – there was a second attacker. That made more sense than a single attacker having four hands. Elliana tried to shake her head to clear the distracting thoughts from her mind, but the attacker still had a firm grip on her mouth.

Elliana had managed to keep her breathing even, however a strange sound from the second attacker caused her chest to involuntarily shiver and her breath to lose its calmness. The little bit of control that Elliana felt was slowly slipping away. A whimper almost managed to escape, but she bit her lower lip and barely held it back.

She could feel it: the radiant heat of her second attacker's presence as they came closer to her face. A pause. The more she noticed it, the longer it felt. She imagined her attackers looking her over, smelling her. For some strange reason, all she could smell were sweet strawberries and sunshine. She loved strawberries.

An unexpected touch on her face jolted her back to the present danger. It took her a moment to understand what her skin was telling her. And then she shivered some more.

She forced her mind to settle down. Elliana needed it clear if she wanted to have a chance to think her way out. She needed to buy time – even if it was just a few precious seconds – to give a chance for help to arrive. The training ground was not far away. Elliana hoped that Vell, the performer, would finish his performance on the training ground and notice something was wrong. What use was training all day if he couldn't help her in her time of need? Elliana silently screamed at the thought of Vell arriving too late to help. Emotions screamed just as loud and almost welled up in her eyes.

But then something stopped her heart cold.

A voice.

The voice of her mounted attacker.

"The way you struggle makes me want to take my time and tease you more," the attacker said with a throaty chuckle.

"Just make her open her mouth so I can shove it in," the second attacker interrupted.

"But she's not going to enjoy it," came the reply.

"I don't care!"

Elliana's eyes shot open with fiery fury. She clamped her mouth shut as tight as she could and thrashed her head and body about. Fear evaporated and was replaced with anger. She recognized their voices!

She felt something strange replace the hand that had covered her mouth. Free to scream, Elliana did not dare open her lips to do so. The attackers continued to press the strange thing into her lips in an effort to get her to open her mouth. But the more they tried, the more she thrashed and resisted. These villains were not going to get away with whatever they were doing, not easily.

The attackers panicked at Elliana's sudden tenacity and they tried to hold her down even more. Elliana fought, but two against one was not a fair fight, especially for someone like her who preferred calm to chaos.

The attackers pinned Elliana's head down.

"Open it!" the main attacker said in frustration. "Open it or else!"

Elliana refused. She tensed her mouth.

A hand reached over to her face.

Elliana braced for it.

But they made an unexpected move. The hand pinched her nose, denying her precious air.

She struggled and struggled, but she knew that it was better for her to live to fight another day than to lose it all.

And finally, she stopped struggling. She opened her mouth and gasped for air. A moment's reprieve was granted. The attackers did not sense a will to struggle any further. They had won.

Then, with a grunt of aggravation, one of the attackers shoved the strange thing into Elliana's mouth. Tears welled up in her eyes. She wasn't sure if it was because of how hard they jammed it in or because of her frustration.

Her tongue touched the strange object. She did not know what disgusting thing these ruffians had shoved into her mouth, so she willed her brain to reject the message. Her brain tried its best, but to no avail. Tears rolled down Elliana's face as she let go of the last bit of resistance.

And the sensations that her brain had been holding back hit her like hurricane.

The taunting voice of her attacker added to the drama. "It's good isn't it?"

Elliana started coughing as she tried to respond.

The attackers tried to pull the thing out of her mouth, but Elliana caught the attacker's hand and gripped it hard, preventing them from removing it.

"Let go!" the attacker said. "You're going to choke on it."

Elliana resisted. Then, with all her might, she bit down – hard.

The attacker screamed as they stumbled back with the remains of the object, splattering its red guts onto attacker's clothes.

The attacker screamed again.

Elliana held a smug expression, bits of red smeared across her face and dribbling down her chin, as she sat up slowly.

The other attacker laughed.

Elliana looked down at herself. She was dirty, her hair was a mess, dress wrinkled and face covered in red. She slowly, and purposefully, chewed on whatever had remained in her mouth. Each time her teeth sunk into it, the deliciousness exploded in her mouth. She savored it, swirling it in her mouth with her tongue, even as the first attacker continued to scream and yell expletives.

And before long, the remnants in her mouth were gone.

And she wanted more.

Elliana looked at the other attacker.

"Don't worry, we've got more," the attacker answered Elliana's silent question.

She didn't care how her friends had gotten ahold of the expensive and often-sold-out pastry, but she did want to know why they felt they needed to terrify her and shove it down her throat.

Lucinda just continued to laugh in her enchanting way as both she and Elliana observed Tatiana smearing the strawberry filling all over her clothes as she tried to get it off. Her face displayed a different type of rage and annoyance as Elliana asked her question.

"I-It's because you were gawking at Vell again," Tatiana stammered. "You literally have drool on your clothes!"

"It's because I nodded off," Elliana shot back. She blushed slightly as she realized that she had no reason to defend herself – she hadn't drooled over her neighbor Vell. Right?

"Well, it pissed me off to see you drooling over that useless idiot Vell," Tatiana said. "After all the effort and hard work we put in to finally get the pastries to surprise you, and then..." She crossed her arms across her chest and just huffed without finishing her sentence.

Hard work? Elliana thought. She felt guilty somehow, even if watching Vell was not wrong. But she remembered that the real reason was probably because Tatiana hated Vell.

And it was understandable, and maybe even well-earned. Vell often kept to himself. And when he did talk to people, it was like he could not understand why people felt so emotional about things. It seemed like he was looking down on everyone because of how cold and logical he acted, but, really, he was just socially awkward. He and his mother had been through a lot during the war that happened almost ten or so years ago. A lot of people had been affected by it. The war had ravaged most of the land. Even after so many years, the effects still lingered, especially in Vell. But no matter the reason for his behavior, it often led to trouble.

"What did you mean by 'hard work'?" Lucinda asked Tatiana.

Tatiana blushed, and answered in a low voice, "You know, the begging and the... flirting."

Lucinda laughed. "That may be hard work for you, but not for me," Lucinda said as she batted her eyes mockingly and turned her head in a way that made her hair flip seductively.

That earned her a jab from Tatiana. "You had to go there!"

"It's not like you're not pretty," Lucinda said, "but you are crass."

"What does that even mean?"

Lucinda exaggerated a sigh. "It means that you're uncultured, unrefined, unladylike... shall I go on?" She made it seem like she was lecturing a child. She held a dramatic pause as she waited for a reply. Hearing none, she continued, "Hooligan? You know, like your brothers?"

"I'm not like my brothers," Tatiana grunted as she hit Lucinda in the arm, the use of violence supporting Lucinda's argument. "Or like my dad!"

Lucinda was right. Tatiana was pretty. Both Tatiana and Lucinda were prettier than Elliana, at least that's what she thought. Tatiana had sharp, prominent features with a head of red hair, cropped at chin's-length, which seemed to blaze in the sunlight. But her temperament, as well as her family's reputation, easily warded off chance of romance. As for Lucinda, it was hard to tell if it was her looks or physique that was attractive, or the way she carried herself. It was also hard to tell if her gaze was one of seduction or of deviousness, but more often than not, it was the latter. Often, she was mistaken as someone older and more mature.

Elliana was always amused at the thought of the two polar opposites being good friends.

And at that, Elliana caught Lucinda giving Tatiana a loud slap. The shocked expression on Tatiana's face said it all: Lucinda would reap a lavish return on that slap. And to that face Lucinda just laughed and laughed.

So maybe they weren't good friends with each other, but they were definitely Elliana's best friends.

Elliana closed her eyes and savored the moment. She felt grateful for the perfect day, her friends, the satisfied feeling of good pastry lingering on her tongue and settling in her belly. Who knew if she would ever feel like this again, and she did not want to take it for granted. She loved her life.

Elliana opened her eyes and looked at herself – her dress was disheveled and her hair a mess, not to mention the sticky mess around her mouth that she had tried to lick off. Why couldn't her friends have given her the pastry in a normal way?

"Ladies!" came a call. It was very unlikely that was to be taken at face value since Elliana was a mess and Lucinda and Tatiana had somehow ended up scuffling in the dirt. Very ladylike indeed.

"Yes, mom?" Elliana answered in her sweetest voice, trying to distract her mother's attention from the mess. Fortunately she didn't need to; her mother was amused by the sight and laughed.

"I'm not even going to ask what is going on," Elliana's mother said, shaking her head. This didn't mean that she didn't want to know what was going on, just that she was not going to ask.

"Hello, Ms. Eliza," the girls said. Tatiana started the explanation that wasn't needed. "We spent days trying to convince the baker's son to hold some of their strawberry pastries for us," she said.

"The ones with that cream filling? The ones that are always sold out?" Ms. Eliza said with a raised eyebrow.

"Yes," Lucinda replied. "Tatiana even flirted with him."

Elliana's mother looked mildly surprised. "Tatiana? Flirting?"

"Well, it wasn't flirting really," Tatiana said, trying to defend herself. "It was more like, asking nicely."

"With batted eyes and a bit of twirling hair," Lucinda added.

Tatiana growled. "Whatever," she said, "we found out he had a huge crush on Elliana anyways. That's what got us the pastries."

"What!?" Elliana said in surprise. She surprised herself by how surprise she was.

"The baker's son is a nice boy," Elliana's mother said thoughtfully as she rubbed her chin.

Elliana did not know if her mother was teasing her or not, but she was not going to take the chance.

"Mom!"

"We finally got the pastries. A fresh batch too," Tatiana continued. "We promised we'd talk him up to Elliana, but then…" she paused to control her emotions, "we saw her drooling over Vell…"

"And Tatiana lost it," Lucinda said with a shrug.

"Yeah, what friend drags her friend in the dirt and threatens them with pastry?" Elliana scolded.

"Ones who care for your wellbeing and future," Tatiana said loudly. "He doesn't even go to school, Elliana, he just plays with his sword all day."

"To be fair," Elliana's mother interjected, "he did try to go to school even though it was very difficult for him."

"Yeah, and then your brothers made it worse by picking on him," Lucinda said knowing she was stoking the flames.

Tatiana threw up her hands. "Well, whatever!" she said. "Those hooligans were the ones to get thrashed anyways. But that doesn't explain skipping school entirely. Get an apprenticeship or something useful. Using your trauma as an excuse can only last so long before it gets stale."

Tatiana crossed her arms in a huff, and an uncomfortable silence settled in.

"And we found out that Tatiana's dad is coming home early," Lucinda said.

Tatiana sighed. "Yes, thanks for pointing that out, Luci."

"Ah, so that means you girls will be joining us for dinner?" Elliana's mother asked with a knowing grin.

Tatiana and Lucinda nodded their heads.

"Did you hear that, Vell?" Elliana's mother called over the wall.

"Hear what?" Vell responded, his face void of any expression. He had walked up the hill by the time Elliana's mother had called him. He was covered in sweat, his shirt drenched, but his demeanor was relaxed and on the border of uncaring. He held his long training sword with the hilt in one hand and the blade resting on his shoulder; on the blade hung a training shield by its straps.

He hopped over the wall in a smooth motion that mirrored the elegance of a dance. As he regained his relaxed posture, he adjusted his grip on the hilt, causing the muscles in his forearm to ripple.

"You won't need to have dinner with us because your mother is coming home early," Elliana's mother responded.

The change in Vell's face was immediate. It flipped from expressionless to the giddy grin of a little boy.

"Really?" Vell asked. Elliana's mother nodded in response.

And just like that, Vell ran off to his house, fumbled with the door and stumbled inside. The clang and clatter of who-knows-what rang throughout the house.

Elliana found herself a little sad that Vell had not even acknowledged her presence before running off. She enjoyed having dinner with him, even if he did not say much.

"Guess we're taking his spot then," Lucinda quipped.

"And Elliana," Tatiana said in a sing-song tone, "wipe that drool off your cheek."

Elliana unwittingly complied, then she realized that her friends were teasing her, again.

She liked Vell, but not like that. She found him interesting. Their families had helped each other out for as long as she could remember. He was just interesting, if you got to know him more. She didn't particularly like him, not in that way... right?

2

Ahead of schedule and with the town in sight, the column dropped from a hard ride to a leisurely trot. Though the conditions on the road had not forced a change in pace, the remainder of the day was too beautiful to waste on pushing a hard ride. And after a successful mission and with the town in view, the mercenaries no longer felt the urgency to rush to their destination. Relaxed, and no longer worried about biting their tongues, the soldiers began to converse amongst themselves – except for the two at the head of the column.

One was a large, muscled man who looked exactly like what one expected a thriving soldier-for-hire to look like. He rode an equally intimidating horse, jet black, covered strategically in armor. The man's heavy armor and large sword contrasted with his shock of deep red hair. His partner at the head of the column was just as much a contrast. She was a lithe and much younger lady who not only looked elegant, but also had the air of it around her. The swords she carried varied in size and design, and her armor favored lightness and speed over heavy protection. Her face had a gentle beauty to it with stark accents; her eyes were a rare, crystal-grey and her hair almost seemed to glow white. The white wasn't one from old age, but rather of an almost-pure form of silverish gold. Her horse happened to be white as well, but it looked almost yellowish in comparison.

Both sat silent and stoic as they lead the column and enjoyed the scenario. But in truth their ears were tuned to the gossip and banter from the troops behind them, the sound of the trotting hooves barely disguising the words.

"You know…," one of the riders mused, "even though Tilian always said that he and Keiara were partners, I just assumed he was being nice and that he was the one actually in charge."

His partner in the column just scoffed but didn't say a word.

"But when those bandits jumped us and tried to free our bounties, well, I've never seen anyone move so fast," the rider said in silent awe. "Or kill so fast."

His partner hocked a nasty spitball towards the side of the road. "That's because you're still a rookie," he said. "She'll kill people if she has too, and she's better than most at it too, but she don't like it none."

His eyes narrowed as he looked at the less experienced mercenary hoping he'd pay attention to his words. "When that kill-switch flips, she's like a whole different person."

The rider gulped hard, partially at his partner's words, but more at the memory of what he had experienced. "It's... scary."

"Damn right it is."

A moment passed as the unsaid words of caution sunk into the younger soldier's soul.

"And you best remember that," the experienced soldier said, hammering it home.

A gentle breeze blew and sent a chill down the soldier's spine. It also seemed to be in sync with the knowing smile that slowly grew on both Keiara and Tilian's faces.

"We made good time," Tilian said. "Looks like we'll be home before dinner." He rolled his shoulders in an attempt to get rid of the stiffness in his muscles.

"Unless you decide to stop for a pint," Keiara quipped.

Tilian smiled at the thought. "I could use one, if yer up for it," he said to his elegant partner.

"No thanks," she replied with a smile. "I'm going home."

Tilian sighed with genuine disappointment. "Aye, I should go home, too," he said. A pint (or more) would've been nice, but Tilian missed his family, especially his feisty daughter, Tatiana. "Alcohol tends to get me into trouble."

Keiara let out a loud, knowing laugh. "Yes, that's how we met, remember?" She loved teasing the bulky, gruff soldier about it.

But Tilian took it in stride, or more accurately, he knew his place. "Of course, lassie, how could I forget?" He chuckled at the memory of him being thoroughly beaten by a young Keiara. The funny thing was she hadn't even been trying very hard. She was new in town and did not want to hurt the people she was trying to be neighbors with.

For Tilian, that is one of his fondest memories. The war had done a number on him and he rolled into a sort of bleakness that permeated into his soul and almost every aspect of his life. The things he had witnessed, and the horrors he had to deal with, slowly sapped his determination and his patriotism away. The Scourge was terrible; these monsters that deformed every living thing they touched were horrible things to see, let alone to fight. However, the real horrors were the people: those who took advantage of the chaos, those who preyed on the weak and desperate, the good people who did terrible things for the sake of survival, or even the good men and women who stood up bravely to fight only for them to make an impact like whispers in a storm, their existence easily extinguished.

Tilian himself had been forced to cut down fellow soldiers who had become greedy, or worse, had become afraid and tried to flee, leaving their comrades behind. And in the midst of this war, bickering politicians had the audacity to put their agendas before the well-being of people, squabbling over matters of insignificance and fighting over resources and territories. Men and women that could've helped turned the tide against the Scourge were instead directed to attack other people, sometimes even those that had been their comrades just moments before.

The disgust built up in Tilian, and when the war finally ended, he was caught in a haze.

Then he picked on Keiara, and she saved his life.

At least that's how he told the story. Keiara had heard multiple variations of it by now. The important thing was that he felt ingratiated to her which allowed them to be good friends instead of enemies.

Tilian turned slightly to face the column. "Alright, lads and lassies," he yelled. "Let's finish this up so we can all go home."

Keiara looked at Tilian with a smirk. "And so you can stop talking like a barkeeper."

"Aye!" Tilian yelled, grinning like a fool.

All Keiara could do was sigh, shake her head, and ride on.

Dusk had settled by the time Keiara made it home. She had gone to the guild hall and dropped off her horse, which deserved a good pampering after that run. Then she bought provisions to last just for the night and the next day's breakfast.

Balancing her gear and groceries, she fumbled with her keys to the house. The lack of light outside did not help. Finally she opened the door. The brightness inside the house rushed out to greet her. The reprieve from the dark had brought a warm smile to her face. Keiara expected a jubilant greeting from her son, Vell. Instead, it was suspiciously quiet. It was as if he had been there and then suddenly left.

Maybe he went next door to have dinner, Keiara thought.

She set down the groceries on the large dining table in the main area of the house. She then set her knapsack on the floor by the door, freeing her arms. The weight off, and the balancing act no longer required, she rolled her shoulders and massaged the muscle between the shoulders and the neck.

She proceeded to put away her swords, shield and other gear but paused.

The atmosphere did not feel right.

In that instant, she pulled out her sword and shield, barely missing the strike. She would've been faster if she had not hesitated for a split second thinking it was Vell trying to hug her.

The attacker had hidden in the darkness of the stairs and had jumped forward to add their weight to the strike. When rebuffed by Keiara's sword and shield, the redirected force had made the attacker summersault backwards.

Keiara's heartbeat jumped from a peaceful pace to full-speed in a moment's notice. Adrenaline rushed through her system. Her senses threw itself wide open to take in any detail. Time seemed to slow down for her.

The attacker landed on the ground only long enough to click his tongue in annoyance. He pulled he sword out and up in a sweeping motion, as if he had unsheathed his sword and attacked in one swift motion.

Keiara parried the attack effortlessly with a half-spin and then fluidly used the momentum to move away from her attacker and get into a better defensive position with her shield held up.

Not a moment too soon, the attacker swept his sword in from the left, colliding into the shield that had not been there just moments before.

Keiara then pushed her shield back against the attacker in an attempt to throw him off balance, but the attacker was already in the middle of another maneuver. His attack attempted to breach the right side, but this time it was blocked by Keiara's sword.

Sensing the frustration, Keiara moved slightly back and to the right, creating an opening and inviting the attacker into her personal space. But the opposite happened: the attacker stumbled forward, thrown off balance.

Keiara used the chance to slam her shield into her opponents face and body, pushing him up into the air and then into the ground. The attacker fell squarely on his hindquarters.

Before the attacker could regain his stance, let alone his composure, Keiara had the tip of her sword in his face. She expected him to yield.

But he didn't.

So Keiara executed a finishing maneuver. She stepped in, flipped her hand around, sword hilt faced down, and bopped the opponent on the crown of his head.

The attacker's face turned into one of pain in the most comical way. "Ow!" he moaned.

Keiara picked up her opponent by the scruff of his shirt and then proceeded to put him in a headlock. She took her fist, knuckles first, and jabbed it into her attacker's head.

"How many times have I told you…" she yelled. "No! Sparing! In the! House!"

Vell continued to whine in pain as he admitted his defeat.

"Okay, okay!"

Keiara looked at her son directly at his face with a stern expression, but she could not keep up the façade for long – she broke into a smile. "It's good to be home," she said. Then she hugged and kissed him on the cheek. "I love you, you little rascal."

"I love you too, mom."

Keiara stood up and held out her hand to help Vell up. "Alright, let's start preparing dinner."

Vell grinned enthusiastically and nodded his head.

It was good to be home.

To one with a normal life, the humdrum of daily chores could be a dull, soul-sucking distraction to the many possible adventures in life. But to one where adventure was a daily necessity, the humdrum was a welcome breath of dull air.

Although Vell did a good job of keeping the house in order while Keiara was away, he often kept the house closed up and most items untouched. So the first thing Keiara did after a mission was air out the house and freshen things up. Laundry for the linens and beddings were a must, even if they were unused. It was surprising what a little kiss of sunshine could do to the fabrics. Then there was the gear to attend to – both hers and Vell's. His training gear often wore down more quickly while she was away.

Eliza, their neighbor caught them just as they were finishing up with their long list of chores.

"Hello Keiara," Eliza, said. "Lovely day, isn't it?"

"It is," Keiara beamed. She took a deep breath to savor the day as if she just noticed it. "It has been nice recently."

"But I'm sure any weather here is nicer than the north's," Eliza said. It was a well-meaning comment, but it spurred a flash of memory that set off a pang of sadness in Keiara's heart. Eliza did not miss the change in countenance that briefly appeared on Keiara's face. "I'm sorry, I shouldn't have said that. I'm sure it was beautiful."

Keiara smiled at Eliza, assuring her. "It's alright. It was beautiful once upon a time, before the war, even in the dead of winter."

The Scourge had come down through the north and carved a large chunk out of the nation as it made its way south. Keiara and Vell's homes were destroyed by the Scourge, which sent them both running. They only stopped running when it was sure that the Scourge had been held back. That's how they found themselves in a perfect, quaint town that had been untouched by the war.

And Eliza and her family were the ones who had helped Keiara and Vell as they settled into the town and worked to recover from the war.

"It does bring back memories," Keiara said with a far-off look, "both good and bad."

"I'm sorry, I shouldn't have brought it up," Eliza said again.

Keiara just shook her head with a smile. "It's okay, really," she said. "It also reminded me of how much you and your family did for us when we first came to town. And I appreciate you all very much."

Ms. Eliza blushed. To her, it was the least she could do. "When you came in with that small boy of yours, and you were barely a child yourself – both of you with faces of pure fatigue and sorrow – we just couldn't help it, dear."

When they had come into town, Keiara was barely sixteen years of age, maybe less, maybe more – the war had made it hard to keep track of time. Vell was just about five or six years of age. Although Vell called Keiara his mother, she was not his real mother. Now it was much harder to tell, since some of their shared northern features made them look close enough to be family, but it had been obvious that the girl that had arrived so many years ago was just taking care of the child she had in tow. Besides, no one in their right mind would've forced such a young girl to have a child that young. But war had brought them together, and they had survived together. And with the horrors that war brought, sometimes they survived things that shouldn't have been a concern during times of normalcy.

And despite the atrocities of war, and the weariness and cautiousness of Keiara and Vell, Eliza's family welcomed them with open arms – and eventually, the town welcomed them as their own.

Feeling better about what she had said, Eliza cheerfully bid her farewells as she prepared to leave the two alone. "Well, I won't keep you. I'm sure you're busy," she said. "I just wanted to make sure you guys were alright."

"Yes, I think we're alright," Keiara responded. "But first, let me get something for you. Please, a second." At that, Keiara went inside the house and, a short while later, reappeared with a small pouch in her hand.

Ms. Eliza knew what it was, and this always made her uncomfortable. However, she has said her piece about it many times. She just smiled a special sort of smile that silently told Keiara that she did not have to, but it was much appreciated.

More importantly, it also said she was not going to argue about it. Out loud, she simply said, "Thank you."

Keiara handed her the bag of currency. The weight suggested more than the usual notes that were used, but the size indicated that the weight of coins would not have made up the bulk of the value. "I know, I know, but I really appreciate you helping and keeping an eye on Vell. And of course, taking care of any trouble he gets into," Keiara said, apologetically.

"Oh, he doesn't get himself into much trouble these days. He mainly keeps to himself."

"Well, consider it interest for the many times he got into trouble when we first arrived," Keiara said with a smile. "And also the food he eats. I know he can eat more than his fair share."

"A growing lad he is," Ms. Eliza said of Vell. He was still fairly slim, but he was well on his way to good growth. "Speaking of which, would you both like to join us for dinner tonight?"

Keiara would normally be hesitant to take such an offer, but she knew the family well and knew they weren't asking out of politeness but a genuine desire to have them over and spend time with them.

"That would be wonderful," she said. "I will have to go to the guild soon to take care of some things, and coming back to one of your dinners would be fantastic."

This delighted Ms. Eliza, of course, and her mind immediately started working overtime to plan what she had to do to, and what she wanted to do for dinner.

"May I accompany you to the guild, Ms. Keiara?" a voice said. It was Elliana. She had overheard part of the conversation between her mother, Eliza, and Vell's mother.

"You want to go to the guild?" Eliza asked, puzzled.

"Yes," Elliana replied cheerfully. "I've always been curious, and it may help me with my decision on what to do after I've completed school."

"My daughter, a mercenary?" Eliza said with mock surprise. "I'm not sure I can imagine that."

"Or Lucinda working in an apothecary," Elliana said, "but there she is."

They laughed at the truth in her statement. Lucinda's family owned an apothecary, so it was natural for her to work there. However, when it came to her personality, well, at least she hasn't killed anyone with her pranks. Yet.

"Vell! Do you want to go to the guild with Elliana and I?" Keiara called into the house. A non-committal sound came out of the house in reply.

Elliana and her mother looked at each other quizzically. Did he want to go or not?

Keiara turned back to the mother and daughter pair. "Okay, we'll head out in a little bit," she said. "Let me clean up a bit and we'll get going."

The guild was housed in a fairly new structure right off the town's common, close to the center of town. It was large and impressive, often the sign of success, or maybe excess. In this case, it was overflowing success – one brought in by the number of well-seasoned veterans who had drifted into town after the war and had decided to stay. A few, like Tilian's family, had already been here well before the war ended.

Before the influx of veterans and skilled hopefuls, the guild was in much more modest accommodations right at the center of town. It was squeezed between an inn and a separate tavern. It made it convenient for visiting travelers and mercenaries to sleep, eat, drink, and get their work done. Not many called the town home. Usually it was just a pit stop before running off on a mission. The guild was still fortunate at the time due to their proximity to a major hub city to the north, Dravenworth. However as the war pushed more and more citizens south, there were those that wanted to get as far south as they could, and did not stop until fatigued forced them to stop at Dravenworth or, if they had enough stamina, make it all the way to this town. And those were few and far-between.

Things seemed to change when Keiara and Vell settled in town. It could've been that they were the agents of change, or that it was a coincidence, but the fact of the matter was that the guild and the town grew tremendously over the past ten years.

Keiara smiled as she watched Elliana's jaw drop and left her mouth in a state that seemed to perpetually say 'wow'. Vell, on the other hand, had been to the guild many times before. His face was as nonchalant as one could be. It portrayed the perfect sense of neutrality, neither expressing positive or negative feelings.

Even if this were his first time, Vell's expression would still be the same, Keiara thought with a mental smirk.

Tilian, as expected, was already in the guild hall, and with a few drinks in him. Tilian noticed Keiara and the kids and called to them loudly, his mug of ale raised.

"Keiara and Vell!" he said, his voice clear over the din. "Wow, and who's this? Elliana in the guild hall!"

Of course, his boisterous call caught the attention of everyone. A loud cheer went up as Keiara walked over to where Tilian sat with his fellow drinking mercenaries.

Elliana slowly wandered over as well, but her focus was on taking in everything she saw.

This prompted a warning from one of the mercenaries as she almost stumbled into a chair. "Watch it, lass," he said. "Better close that mouth before a fly goes in."

Elliana blushed as she realized her state. She quickly closed her mouth and greeted the group.

"Just you, Elliana? No Tatiana?" Tilian asked.

"Just me," she said.

Someone quipped, "Your daughter avoiding you again?"

Tilian just sighed to the group's laughter.

"Is the guildmaster in?" Keiara asked.

Tilian sat up, excitement in his eyes, and said, "Yes he is, and there's a really great mission that's come through."

Considering that they had just come back from a mission, Keiara was not as excited as Tilian. She wanted to enjoy time at home with Vell. The reason she went on missions was to help pay the bills. Of course, the side effect of that was she kept her skills sharp. Sometimes she even helped people who truly needed help, which was great. But she didn't do it for fun or out of desperation.

"I'm not sure I'm interested in a mission just yet," Keiara said. "I just need to talk with the guildmaster about our last mission."

"I'm right here," a voice said from behind her.

"Hello Guildmaster Wyatt," Keiara said. The kids greeted him as well.

"So," the guildmaster turned to the kids and said, "are you both here to check out the guild?"

"I am," Elliana said. "I have never been inside the guild hall before."

"Well Vell has been here plenty of times, I'm sure he could show you around," Keiara said.

And with that, the kids took off to explore – or rather Elliana dragged Vell off to explore.

"It's great that kids have an interest in being a working soldier," the guildmaster mused. "Vell is very talented, and almost of age, if I recall."

Keiara didn't quite like the thought of Vell becoming a mercenary. He had a future and could do anything he wanted. But to see him on the battlefield again...

"So what is this business about you not wanting to go on this mission?" the guildmaster said, interrupting Keiara's thoughts.

"Yeah, it's a big mission," Tilian said.

"What do you mean?"

"Word came in a day or so ago," the guildmaster said. "A government rider arrived with a contract for a training mission for one of their battalions."

A huge contract like this usually went to the guilds in the big cities like Dravenworth. It was unusual for a dedicated rider to come to the guild to deliver it. Usually it would trickle down to through the normal mail routes. People who post the contracts would want the posting to be reviewed by a lot of guilds and mercenaries, so they prioritized the big cities. Regional or special contracts were the ones that usually ended up in the smaller guilds. But it wasn't unusual for Keiara's guild to receive specialized contracts due to the concentration of war veterans and skilled operators in her town.

Still, it didn't make sense to Keiara.

"Why was the contract offered to us?" she said. "Is it a specialist mission?"

"We've got the skills and the veterans of course," Tilian said with a huge grin.

Keiara knew something was off. Tilian was trying to oversell it. He normally did, but even then, something in his demeanor was off. Keiara had been around Tilian for a long time, and he wasn't exactly a difficult man to read.

Tilian's unconvincing smile slowly faded away as he observed the expression on Keiara's face.

"Tilian is partially correct," the guildmaster said. "However, the real reason, I believe, was unsaid – the mission is a long-term training mission at Fort Holden in Hauxville. They'll be back in about a week to evaluate the members."

That explained Tilian's strange demeanor. Fort Holden was right next to passage through the Wall.

The Wall was built to help keep the Scourge at bay. It was an extension of various natural barriers and ancient defensive walls connected to close off the entire northwestern region that had been overrun by the Scourge. The Wall had some sort of repulsive magic that kept the Scourge from getting close to it. The Wall was sealed and all the territory behind the Wall had been abandoned to the Scourge.

People had faith in the Wall; they did not have any choice. And when the Wall held the Scourge back, the people's faith in the magic grew. Keiara, as relieved as she was when the Wall held, did not put all her faith in it. She had good reason not to.

But it seemed that something was going to happen at the Wall, if it had not happened already. Many of the veterans in town had fought or at least seen the horrors of the Scourge up close. However, most of the newer mercenaries had not, and it was almost a certainty that the current crop of government soldiers had not.

In any case, it was bad news, and Keiara did not want to have anything to do with it.

"No, thank you," she said curtly. "Let me get the payment from my missions, and I'll leave you guys to your planning."

"I told you she won't go for it," Tilian said to the guildmaster.

The guildmaster sat down and sighed. "I know, but I can't have the guild go on a mission like this without my two star members," he said before sighing again.

Keiara felt bad, but she did not want to chance an encounter with the Scourge. She had fought them, more times than she'd care to remember, and if someone planned on doing something stupid, she wanted Vell and herself to be as far away as possible so they could get a head start running.

"I've got Vell to think about," was all Keiara managed to say.

"Take the boy with you!" one of the other mercenaries suggested. "It is a training mission after all, and you can continue training him while making money."

It wasn't just leaving Vell behind or the money that worried her. But it was difficult to explain the real reason she wanted to stay away from the Wall. There were secrets she needed to keep, especially secrets involving Vell. Somehow, even Vell had forgotten about his past – and Keiara would prefer to keep it that way. The trauma he had endured and the horrors they had to witness, he was still affected by them even if his mind had wiped it from his consciousness.

Keiara glanced at Vell. He was on the other side of the guildhall, near a training area, gently sparring with Elliana with wooden swords. Memories flashed across her mind's eye, and her inner mind resonated with the voice of a young Vell softly telling her, his mommy, that he was scared. Keiara had to take a moment to compose herself again before she could safely talk without betraying her thoughts.

The group continued to talk about the mission. The young ones were thinking of possible action, while the older veterans were thinking of an easy payday with a chance to bully some government slackers. The guildmaster mentioned something about being able to retire comfortably with the commission. They all had their reasons for this mission to go forward.

But Keiara was firm. She was not risking it. She needed to protect Vell.

"I'm out," she said curtly. "Guildmaster Wyatt, if you would be so kind as to give me my payment. I would like to attend to other matters."

The guildmaster moaned again, keeping the mood light – or so he thought. "Oh, but I can't move the mission forward without you."

"I'm sorry, but you'll have to," Keiara said. "You have more than enough volunteers for the mission."

"But you're the best soldier on the roster!" the guildmaster said. "And besides, you have the most experience fighting the Scourge."

Keiara tensed. Then she turned to look at the guildmaster. She was normally friendly and cordial, but the look she unconsciously gave the guildmaster caused his jovial smile to quickly fade away. No one was joking here.

Catching herself, Keiara closed her eyes and forced her coldness away. When she opened her eyes again, she did so with a warm smile. However, the message had been sent and received clearly. The 'warm smile' made the whole situation even more terrifying for those on the receiving end.

Tilian sighed, his fake enthusiasm melted away. "If you're not going, I'm not going," he said. This almost sent the guildmaster into a tizzy. He recollected what little composure he had left and, again, stated seriously that he could not go forward with the mission without her and Tilian.

Keiara did not care. At least that is what she thought. But her heart softened a bit and her mind continued to fight against her emotions, her fear.

"J-Just promise me you'll think about it," the guildmaster said. Then he walked off to get Keiara her payment.

Keiara sighed. There was not a lot to think about.

3

Elliana had never been inside the mercenary guild before. Sure, she had been outside—it was basically a local tourist attraction – but not inside. And the inside was even more impressive than the outside. The ceilings were high, the space was huge and open, and all sorts of strange decorations caught her sight: from awards and trophies, to trinkets from village vendors and reminders of battles won. It was too much for a simple girl like her to take in. But of course Vell had seen it all, or at least acted like he had.

They met Mr. Tilian, who was Tatiana's father, as well as Guildmaster Wyatt and some of Ms. Keiara's friends. It was all a blur to Elliana until she realized that she was alone with Vell, walking through the different 'exhibits'. Despite his disinterest, it seemed that he had been explaining about the different items that he saw Elliana looking at. Most of it had not registered in Elliana's mind, but when she realized that Vell had been paying attention to her, and even saying more than two words to her, her heart skipped a beat.

"...and they only brought the claw back because they did not want to drag the carcass for three days to the closest town with a delivery service," Vell said.

Elliana realized that she had been staring at some sort of wolf's foot but the size of a cow's head.

"T-That's interesting," she offered.

Vell paused and looked directly into Elliana's eyes. It was a look that stared into her soul. Somehow this made Elliana blush and her heart beat faster. She questioned herself, asking if she had any secrets that she did not want Vell to find out. Consciously, no, but her mind kept telling her otherwise. Her neck stiffened. She tried to turn away and avert his gaze, but she couldn't.

"Do you want to see the training equipment?" Vell said after observing her. "It's where I usually hang out when I'm here."

"S-Sure," she stuttered. Maybe he was just trying to sense if she found his explanations boring.

They walked to an area near the back of the main hall. There were racks and walls filled with all sorts of weapons and devices used, supposedly, in training. Unlike the decorative ones all over the guild hall, these looked like they were for actual use. But Vell picked a worn wooden sword from a bucket sitting on the floor off to the side.

"Here," he said, holding the wooden sword by its blade end and presenting the hilt end to Elliana.

When she took the wooden sword, Vell took another for himself.

"En garde," Vell said in a monotonous tone.

Puzzled, Elliana just looked at Vell. But suddenly, Vell hit the sword in her hand with his sword. After a moment of shock, Elliana turned to glare at Vell, but noticed his raised eyebrow beckoning her to do something. It took a moment for Elliana to realize what that 'something' was, and it took yet another moment for her to figure out how to do it. Somewhere in that moment, Vell landed another hit on her sword. It was slightly less gentle than the previous hit, but it still felt like a tease than a real hit. And it added to her annoyance, ever so slightly.

"Do you find this fun?" she said, her eyes tinged with the lack of amusement.

"Yes."

Elliana sensed a smirk hiding underneath his expressionless face, almost like the smirk his mother sometimes had – one that looked like she was trying to hide but came out anyways.

She lunged out and hit Vell on his thigh with her sword. Vell moved just enough to soften the blow, but mostly the surprise attack worked because Elliana was inexperienced.

"You're supposed to hit the sword," Vell said as he rubbed his thigh. Elliana knew very well that it did not hurt. His mouth twitched and she knew for sure that he was hiding a smirk. He hit him again, this time on the other side.

Despite the foul-play by Elliana, Vell did not reciprocate. He continued to hit Elliana's sword, and Elliana hit back, wherever she could, but she made sure not to hit the face or other sensitive areas. Before they knew it, they were both hitting each other in a flurry with Elliana giggling away and Vell occasionally making funny noises.

Elliana had to call a stop to their sparring when she couldn't breathe anymore due to the combination of laughing too much and moving more than she had in a long time.

"Are you hurt?" Vell asked when Elliana sat down on a bench.

"No, just winded."

After a long pause, Vell answered. "You need to exercise more," he said.

Elliana scrunched her face to hold back a harsh retort. Instead, she said, "Thanks, for stating the obvious."

Somehow, Vell found it amusing. "You are welcome," he shot back. Then he plopped down right next to Elliana on the bench.

The closeness made Elliana suddenly very aware of the sweat she had worked up, and the possible accompanying smell. She felt paralyzed: she did not want to check if she smelled, but at the same time, she did not want to suddenly move away from Vell and make it look like she did not want him sitting next to her.

"Are you okay?" Vell asked.

Elliana turned her head and saw Vell staring right at her. Her neck locked up as she forced herself to turn away. "I-I'm okay," she stuttered, hoping it was more convincing to him than it was to herself.

She mentally shook her head. *What is the big deal?* she thought. When Vell helped her with her schoolwork, he often sat next to her. A thought flashed across her mind, *Maybe it's because of what Tatiana said yesterday.*

Suddenly, Elliana felt a gentle touch on her shoulder. The fingers lingered there while the rest of the hand settled on the part between her neck and shoulders. Her spine tingled, and not in a good way.

Her neck creaked as she turned to look at Vell. "V-Vell, what are you doing?" she managed to ask.

Vell turned to look at Elliana with his head tilted in question. Then Elliana saw his eyes look up above her.

"Yes, Vell," said a voice, "what are you doing?"

"Sitting," Vell answered.

Elliana turned around and looked up. She was greeted by a strikingly attractive girl with a sly smile on her lips and a suspicious look in her eyes. Her neckline led to a shoulder that jutted out slightly and down to an arm with the lean and curvy look of a feminine woman with subdued power. That arm led to the hand gently caressing Elliana's shoulder. The caress did not feel like one of gentle loving care but one of dominance.

"Are you sure you're not flirting," the girl said without taking her eyes off of Elliana. The girl looked like she was smiling, but it did not feel like she was smiling.

"I don't think I was flirting," Vell said. "She's a friend from next door, Elliana."

The girl took her hand off of Elliana's shoulder and offered it to her. "A pleasure to meet you," the girl said, emphasizing the word 'pleasure'. "I'm Miranda, but you can call me Mira."

"Nice to meet you," Elliana replied.

"And this is my cousin Bernard," the girl said as she pointed to a boy that Elliana had not noticed. He just nodded at Elliana with a half-smile, and Elliana nodded back.

"You can lay off, Mira," he said.

"Lay off what?" Mira said with a shrug of feigned innocence. "I'm just checking in with the love of my life." She proceeded to put her arms around Vell and pushed the side of her face into his.

The scene made Elliana blush.

"You just love me for my body," Vell said, expressionless.

As if to emphasize Vell's statement, Mira softly ran her hand over his chest. "What's wrong with that? You enjoy me too," she said in a near-whisper.

Elliana couldn't stand it; she had to cover her face with her hands and block out the sight.

She could hear Mira chuckling seductively and Bernard snickering like a little schoolboy who saw something he was not supposed to.

"So," Mira continued, "do you want to do it?"

The word 'it' sent Elliana's imagination into all sorts of territory. *What are they talking about!?* She screamed internally.

"But I'm here with Elliana," Vell replied.

"Oh, she can watch us... if she wants."

"I like watching too," Bernard said. He snickered again. Mira chuckled in response.

"Do you want to watch, Elliana?" Vell asked.

"Look at her," Mira said, "she's still hiding behind her hands. She's so innocent. I bet she has no experience at all." The last sentence was drawn out and then punctuated with a sing-song voice.

"How do you know?" Vell asked.

"Because of her actions... and her body," Mira answered.

Elliana couldn't stand it anymore. She was about the blow. She put her hands down and balled them into fists. She clenched her jaw. Her heart thumped harder and harder.

But then she closed her eyes tight and took a deep breath to help calm her nerves and her heart. Getting angry here would do nothing for her. She finally managed to calm down, but then something made her heart skip a beat.

"So, do you want to do it?" Vell asked Mira. "But we'll have to be quick. My mother is here."

"I guess I'll have to go all out from the start, or else I won't be satisfied," Mira said with a smirk.

"Okay, then let's just go to the usual place where no one else will disturb us," Vell said before walking off.

"Are coming to watch us go at it, Elliana?" Mira said in her sing-song voice. Then she laughed as she followed Vell somewhere beyond the main guild hall.

Elliana had to go. She was not going to leave Vell alone with this girl.

She followed the path that Vell and Mira took through a darkened hallway, but it did not take long for her to lose their trail. The unfamiliar surroundings disoriented her. However, Bernard eventually caught up to Elliana and led her to the so-called 'usual place'.

Elliana's hand hovered on the doorknob unable to turn it. She looked at Bernard who now wore a serious face. She asked him, "Do you really enjoy watching them… do it?"

He smiled, but there was not a hint of maliciousness or perversion. "It's not for everyone," he said, "but I always enjoy it."

Elliana turned her attention back to the doorknob and gulped. As she got closer, she heard Mira and Vell already at it. The pace and effort seemed furious. Elliana's heart sunk. She couldn't stop her mind from building an image to accompany the sounds beyond the door. Her hand grasped the doorknob. However, she could not bring herself to open the door. She did not want to see the image in her mind brought to life. But she needed to help Vell. Eventually, she gathered her courage, just enough to tip over to action from inaction, and opened the door.

Immediately the heat and musk from inside the room rushed out and hit Elliana like a solid wall. It hit her so hard that she had to close her eyes and turn her head away. The sound hit her next; the fury of ecstatic grunts and moans was much louder with the door open.

Bernard rushed in past her. Elliana turned her head just in time to see a topless Vell being rammed against the wall by Mira.

"Wow! You guys are really going at it," Bernard yelled with a whoop.

"He said we needed to be quick," Mira replied. "Now stop distracting me!"

Something flashed across Elliana's vision, then something else, and then more. Vell and Mira's bodies moved like a blur, and then they tumbled out of view. But Elliana noticed something: Mira was almost fully clothed, save for her light jacket.

Elliana wasn't really sure how 'that' worked, but either Mira was in such a rush that she left most of her clothes on, or that 'it' was not what she thought it was.

She stepped further into the room.

And she saw Vell do a back-flip off the wall and spin in mid-air to both avoid Mira and strike her at the same time.

"Look at them go," yelled Bernard to no one in particular.

It was obvious. It wasn't 'it' – 'it' was sparring.

Elliana had a hard time following Vell and Mira's movements. Although Elliana had watched Vell trained at the training grounds more times than she could count, this fight was something entirely different. The graceful flourishes were still there, but it was more hardened and fiercer.

Bernard, after observing Elliana's face, offered, "They are using blunted weapons weighted to feel like real ones. They'll be okay."

"Oh…" Elliana replied.

"I mean, it will still hurt if they get hit," Bernard said, then added, "but Vell hardly ever gets hurt… it's mostly Mira."

Elliana turned to look at Bernard incredulously. "You mean Mira loves doing this even if she gets hurt?"

"Oh yeah, she loves sparring with Vell," he said. "Everyone else bores her, including me."

"Even the more experienced soldiers?" Elliana asked.

Bernard laughed. "They don't want to deal with this type of mess," he said. "Mira is too wild, and they don't want to get hurt unnecessarily."

"And Vell does?"

"Well," Bernard paused as he gathered his thoughts. "Vell usually does not get hurt. He's also not very picky about who he spars with." Bernard paused again, his hand to his chin. "You know, I think he adjusts to fit the person his spars. When I spar with him, I feel significantly challenged but not overwhelmed. On the other hand, he can give Mira a challenge even though she's much better than me."

He turned to Elliana and asked, "Do you get what I mean?"

Not really, she thought.

"I think so," she said.

A loud thump and accompanying groan brought their attention back to the fight.

Mira was on the floor holding her back, cursing a storm. Vell, ever the warrior, held firm in a cautious stance. Elliana wondered if she should help Mira or if Vell thought the fight was not over.

"Are you done, Mira?" Bernard asked.

She pounded her fist on the floor. "Yes, damn it!"

Bernard mumbled an expletive and rushed to help her. "Satisfied?"

"Yes!" Mira yelled. "Now shut up, Bernard!"

Bernard smirked as he helped Mira off the floor. "I thought you liked it rough."

"I do!" she yelled while holding her back.

Elliana turned to Vell who had finally relaxed his stance. "Did you have to be so rough?" she asked.

"She likes it rough," he deadpanned.

Elliana just stared at him incredulously.

It seemed like he got the hint and moved over to Mira. He asked her to show him her back, and then he ran his hands over it as if he were searching for something with his fingers. He finally found something and pressed it, soliciting another groan from Mira.

Then Vell did something with his fingers and jabbed her in the spot. This solicited another groan, louder this time, which slowly morphed into a long, disturbingly ecstatic moan with cackling spattered in.

Strangely enough, this made Bernard visibly uncomfortable. He still held Mira, but just barely. His grip had slipped over the course of her ecstasy.

This amused Elliana, just a bit. She, of course, held any indication of it in.

Vell had left Mira writhing as soon as he completed his weird hand-to-back motion on her.

"Come on, Elliana," he said without emotion, "I'm sure my mother is done by now."

Elliana, Vell and his mother left the guild and continued to run their errands. The next stop was the bank. Vell's mother deposited her earnings from her work and even gave Vell some to put into his account.

Elliana had not really considered opening an account with the bank. It was seen as something adults did, and only those who really had money. She also did not quite understand how the banking system worked. It was amazing that someone who had money in a bank in one town could access the same account in another town. But most things that used High Technology magic were unexplainable.

However, seeing that Vell had an account of his own made her want to have one too. She asked questions and the nice tellers replied as simply as they could. Vell helped explain things occasionally when it was too difficult to understand. Elliana was always amazed at how Vell's answers often sparked something in her brain that gave her clarity.

"Do you want to open an account?" the teller said to Elliana.

It tempted Elliana. Setting one up was relatively straight-forward, and they had already helped walk Elliana through filling in the documents. Having an account would make her feel more adult-like and, of course, more like a higher member of society instead of just a normal family like she was from.

"If you'd like, I could put some money in to start your account," Vell said.

"But isn't it your money?" Elliana asked. "Don't you need to keep it for yourself?"

"Money is just money," Vell replied.

Only the rich can say that, Elliana thought with a momentary feeling of jealousy and insignificance. She shook her head to clear out the nasty thoughts. Vell didn't deserve that.

Vell took that as a 'no'.

"Are you sure?" he said. "The money is for me to use on what is important, and you're important to me, so I would be happy to help you with the account minimum." He was referring to the minimum amount of money needed for someone to open an account. It must've been a way to prevent too many people from taking up the bank's time with their meager savings.

Her head resonated with what he said, how important she was to him, and it took her awhile to get her thoughts straight again. But when she did, she politely declined the offer to open the account. She didn't think she'd ever be rich enough to use it, and she did not want to burden Vell by using his money.

"That's okay," the teller said with a smile. "You've filled out the proper information, so just come back with the paperwork and the minimum balance and we can open an account for you."

"T-Thank you," Elliana muttered. She felt like she had wasted the teller's time. Even so, she clutched the paperwork tightly before stuffing it into her pocket.

"You should keep that information safe," Vell said. "Someone could use it to open a bank account."

"Why would anyone want to do that?" Elliana said.

"There are reasons, but still it is better to keep it safe," he said.

She fished the formerly-pristine form from her pocket and gave it to Vell. "Can you keep it for me?"

"Sure," he said. He then took the paper and put it in his pocket.

Somehow, it felt like a burden had been lifted off of Elliana. It's like she had been so troubled by reaching for the stars when all she had to do was remind herself of reality and be satisfied with it.

My life is fantastic, she thought. *There's no need to be greedy for more.*

They continued running their errands and enjoying their day around town. Vell even bought Elliana a small bag for her to put things in so she did not have to shove them into her pockets. He may have felt like he had to get her something in place of the bank account. It made Elliana happy. And by the time they were done, it was time for dinner.

The sun had set and the walk back was caught between the time of natural light and light from the street lamps. Elliana entered the house first.

"Welcome home, Elliana," her mother said. Elliana responded in kind. Then her eyes adjusted to the low-lit room and noticed that her friends, Tatiana and Lucinda, were there.

They jumped up to greet her and hug her happily.

"What are you guys doing here?" Elliana asked.

"What do you think?" Tatiana said with a playful pout. She obviously wanted to avoid her dad.

Elliana turned to Lucinda. "What about you? Just tagging along?"

Lucinda gave a sheepish smile. "Parents went on a business trip or a 'trade expedition' as they call it. I ran before they could make me watch the store."

"Well, you are both very welcome, anytime," Elliana's mother said.

The girls started chattering endlessly, as if they had not seen each other in years.

But suddenly Tatiana's smile fell off her face. Lucinda noticed first and turned around to look at where Tatiana's eyes laid as her smile fell.

"Oh my," Lucinda said, putting a hand to her mouth.

Elliana turned as well. "Oh, yeah... this will be fun," she said as she turned back to Tatiana and smiled.

"Hello Eliza," Vell's mother said as she walked through the door. She held a basket of goodies that she had bought while running errands.

And Tatiana knew that if Vell's mother was here, that means Vell was not far behind. Sure enough, Vell walked in right after his mother, hands in his pockets.

Elliana saw that Tatiana had frozen. Whether it was out of hatred or fear, Elliana could imagine her mind running through all her options.

"Tati, are you okay?" Lucinda said in a low, sing-song voice.

Tatiana, who hated when people called her Tati, did not react to Lucinda's verbal jab.

"Hello, girls," Vell's mother said. "Will you be joining us for dinner?"

Tatiana stammered. It almost sounded like she wanted to say no. But Lucinda cut her off before she could answer.

"Yes we are, Ms. Keiara," Lucinda answered in the sweetest voice. Vell's mother patted Lucinda on the head like a good, sweet girl would deserve, but Elliana had the feeling that Vell's mother was not so easily taken in by Lucinda's sweetness.

Ms. Keiara turned to Vell and said, "Vell, be sure to greet Elliana's friends."

"Hello," Vell said curtly before turning away. He moved to help set up the table. He had eaten at Elliana's house often enough to know where everything was and develop a routine.

The monotonous response garnered a chuckle out of Lucinda, but a 'humph' with crossed arms from Tatiana.

"Will father be joining us?" Elliana asked her mother.

"He should be here shortly, but we can start without him."

Elliana and her friends moved to help with the finishing touches of the meal and setting the table. Her father often came home late as the seasons needed. But she was glad that she was still able to spend a bit of time with him in the mornings before she went off to classes or to venture out with her friends. More importantly, she was thankful that her father did not have to go off for long periods of times like the mercenaries. There were a lot of families who did not see certain members for long periods of time, such as Vell and his mother.

Finally, they sat down and had their dinner. For the most part there was the usual chatter and polite-talk. Elliana's mother asked Vell's mother for the details of her trip, and Vell's mother happily obliged. Meanwhile, the girls kept relatively quiet: Tatiana, because she did not want to really say anything in front of Vell, and the other two, because they were having fun at Tatiana's expense. Vell, as usual, kept to himself and just ate dutifully.

The main course eventually ran its course and the rewards were presented: dessert and hot drinks.

"So Elliana, did you have fun at the guild today?" her mother asked.

"You went to the guild!?" Lucinda gasped. She had been to the guild once before, when she was a little girl, and had always wanted to go back.

Elliana nodded, answering both her mother and Lucinda. "It was interesting, and I even got to see a sparring match," she said.

"Ooh," Vell's mother exclaimed. "Who did you see?"

"Vell and Mira."

Ms. Keiara had a knowing look on her face. "Vell against Mira, huh," she said with a smile. "Who won?"

"Vell did," Elliana responded.

"She kept on teasing Elliana," Vell interjected without taking his eyes off his cup.

"What did she tease you about?" Vell's mother asked.

Elliana's face turned a brilliant red at the memory. Vell's mother laughed and said, "Oh, never mind. Knowing Mira, I can guess what it was about."

"What? What!?" Lucinda asked excitedly.

"N-Nothing," Elliana said as she looked down in an effort to conceal her embarrassment.

Lucinda begged and begged for an answer, but Elliana refused.

"And where did you get the bag from?" Lucinda said. "From a secret admirer?"

"N-No," Elliana stammered, "Vell bought it for me."

Tatiana suddenly started laughing loudly. "It sounds like you had a grand ole time with Vell," she said sarcastically. "Almost sounds like..." Tatiana paused, and then she lit up like a firecracker. "...like a date!"

A date!?

"No, it wasn't a date!" Elliana retorted.

"Oh, it definitely was a date," Tatiana said.

"No, it wasn't," Elliana said, more conviction in her voice than in her mind.

Tatiana started counting on her fingers. "You guys went out, had fun, he even bought you an expensive bag..." she paused dramatically and looked at them carefully. "...should I say more?"

Elliana could not process all the information that had been laid out in a different light. Conflict and confusion roiled in her mind. She liked Vell, a lot, but not like that... or did she? Maybe others could see what she could not see. Maybe they had a better perspective. It was her friend who kept saying it and maybe she was the only one willing the voice to truth. But Elliana did not know – not for certain.

And then Lucinda saved her from her agony.

"You're just jealous that she's gone on dates and you haven't," Lucinda said to Tatiana.

Tatiana's facial expressions changed from one extreme to the other very quickly.

"W-What? I'm not jealous," she said with an angry scowl. "Why would I be jealous of Elliana going on a date with Vell?"

"Oh, such innocence," Lucinda said. It was obvious that she was stoking the flames on purpose.

It worked, and Tatiana exploded like a cluster of fuel bombs. The quiet after-meal quickly turned into a ruckus worthy of the most base pub or tavern.

Tatiana's face matched the color of her red hair as she yelled and shouted. Lucinda shouted back, but her face held a sinister, gleeful grin as her words cut down Tatiana's angry defense and prodded her further into fury. Elliana's pleas for calm fell on deaf ears. The spectators meanwhile sighed and continued to sip their drinks as they observed the row so as to intervene if it became too much.

Vell, on the other hand, completely ignored the argument like it was just a normal conversation – one that he was not even remotely associated with – and kept on eating his dessert pastry and slowly sipping his drink.

But he was the first to notice when the door opened.

"Wow, sounds like my kind of night!" Elliana's father said as he walked in. He set down his bundle at its place near the door and proceeded to undo his work boots. "Are there still leftovers from the party?"

"Of course, dear," Elliana's mother said. She then went off to prepare the food that they had set aside for him.

He greeted everyone and sat down at the table. The earlier ruckus had turned to an awkward silence. But Elliana's father did not seem bothered by it. After settling in, he started discussing things with Vell's mother. Elliana's mother occasionally added her thoughts. Overall, the conversation seemed to be the usual adult stuff; beyond the concerns of the kids who were stuck arguing about dates and appearances.

Elliana felt embarrassed. Lucinda, on the other hand, had the face of a victor while Tatiana had the opposite.

But Vell's disinterest during the commotion had turned to interest in what the adults were talking about. Elliana did not understand what was being said. The individual words had meaning, but not when strung together in sentences. It was almost like they were talking in a secret language.

The secret language was even harder to decipher once Elliana's father started stuffing his face with food.

"Slow down, dear, or you'll choke on your food," Elliana's mother warned.

Elliana's father stopped and took a big gulp. "Sorry, it's just so good," he said. Then he turned to Vell and asked, "Are you interested in all this land management stuff we're talking about, Vell?"

"A little bit, I guess," Vell answered.

"Is that something you want to do?" Elliana's father said. "You're almost of age, and that's really because of school. You could actually start working soon." He took another big bite, but chewed more meaningful this time. "You know, you could even start tomorrow if you wanted."

"Oh, don't pressure the boy," Elliana's mother said.

"I'm not!" he said in fake protest and a mouth full of food. "But it would be great to have a strapping, young man helping with the work. It's with your family's help that we even have the opportunity." Elliana's father winked at Vell, and Vell responded with a small smile.

"Well, we appreciate your help," Vell's mother said. "I don't think I could be at ease leaving Vell behind if it weren't for you all."

"More than happy to help," Elliana's mother said. There was an obvious non-verbal exchange between her and Vell's mother. The things she would always say were left unsaid but still implied. Vell's mother understood and nodded her head.

"Grateful for the investment advice too," Elliana's father said after gulping down his drink. "It's amazing how complicated these things seem when you don't know what is going on."

That's the whole thing about education, Elliana mused as her father summarized it all neatly into one sentence. Elliana was almost done with school, but there was still so much that she did not know. Wasn't she supposed to be an almost-grownup already?

"So what do you want to do, Vell," Elliana's father said.

Vell shrugged as his face was covered by the cup he was trying to drain. He put it down and gave a proper answer. "I don't know... maybe a mercenary like my mother, or something."

"That is... something," Elliana's father said cautiously. Maybe there was a bit of disappointment in his voice too.

"He's really committed to his training." Elliana's mother said. "I see him out by the tree training all the time, and he's a smart boy. He's often helping Elliana with her school work."

Elliana had to agree. Either she was not very good at school work, or Vell knew a lot about school for someone who did not go to school.

"And I saw him spar with someone in the guild," Elliana said. "He is really good."

Elliana glanced at Vell and found him looking at her. "Thanks," he said softly before turning his eyes away.

"You were at the guild?" Elliana's father exclaimed. "Don't tell me you want to be a mercenary too," he moaned.

"N-No," Elliana stammered. The image of her being a mercenary, bumbling along with people like Mr. Tilian and Mira, was not a pretty one. "I just accompanied Vell and Ms. Keiara to the guild."

"I didn't mean it like that, Eliana," her father said. "You can do what you think is best… maybe." He looked up at the ceiling thoughtfully, then shook his head and brought his thoughts back to reality. "But I would miss my daughter very much if she was always far from home."

Even though Elliana had no thoughts of becoming a mercenary before her father had mentioned it, she still appreciated his sentiments. "Thanks, dad," she said with a smile.

And it was only then that Elliana noticed the dark, aimless expression on Ms. Keiara's face.

4

Keiara had a hard time sleeping. Her mind swirled with all the information and issues, searching for a solution. Every time she had figured out something that may work, more information and more worries came in. She had already given up hope of a perfect solution, but she at least wanted a satisfactory one.

The mission near the Wall troubled her a lot. Whether she liked it or not, she somehow had become one of the people that the town and her guildmates looked up to. Many of the guild members were excited to go for an easy mission, especially one where they had the power to bully the army for once. But she did not like it. The Scourge was too close. If anything happened, the mercenaries would be the first ones to get hit. She wouldn't be able to run with Vell.

And Vell was another worry. He's 15 years old – almost 16 – an age where most kids would be looking forward to the rest of their lives. Some start even younger if they did not go to school like Vell. To be fair Vell already knew most of the things that they taught in the local school. He was required to learn it long ago when they were up in the north. And because he had not been able to enjoy his childhood or learn basic social interactions, like most of the kids in this town had a chance to, he ended up keeping to himself. When he did talk to others, he had a difficult time because he did not understand why they would fuss about things that seemed so small and inconsequential. He did not understand that some of those things were important to kids and was a big part of their world. To him, it was like a little child arguing with a senior instructor: not worthy of the instructor's time or attention.

But Keiara could not really blame the boy for his social immaturity. She was the one that encouraged it. Sure, it was because they were on the run. They did not know who to trust, who would take advantage of them, or who would even help them. And those were the dangerous ones. A bond would be formed, and sacrifice or betrayal could result from that bond, neither of which was good. The emotional strength that they needed to persevere, to survive, would have been torn away by each result of a bond. The bonds had to be tight. Vell was the only one that mattered. She had to protect Vell at all cost. Her partner, affectionately referred to as Vell's father, had already paid the price. And the mental strain of that bond breaking was more than Vell could handle.

He was not Vell's real father, as much as Keiara was his real mother. She had not even met Vell's real parents – only seen them in passing. Keiara had developed strong feelings for the man. Not the romantic type of feelings, though she did struggle with the distinction in the beginning, but one of camaraderie and brotherhood. But...

Keiara slammed her fist into her thigh. The gentle soreness took her mind off of the thing she could do nothing about and brought it back to what she may be able to do something about. A sigh escaped her lips as she thanked herself for not slamming her fist against the table top. It would've either spilled her drink or made the cup jump high enough to risk breaking and waking Vell up.

Vell...

"What am I going to do with him?" she said to herself in a whisper.

She knew that her life was dedicated to protecting him. That's what she was brought up to do, trained to do, even if he was not her initially assigned to her. That didn't matter. Their past did not matter, nor the reasons why they were here. All that mattered was protecting Vell – keeping him safe.

However, after they escaped to this town and eventually settled here, her guard had lowered and she created bonds: bonds with neighbors, bonds with the townsfolk, bonds with her guildmates, and bonds with fellow veterans and refugees who had experienced the war in close proximity. She knew going to the Wall was a bad idea. Treading anywhere close to the Scourge was a bad idea. If anything were to happen, and there was a good chance of that, then Keiara wanted to be as far away as possible with Vell so they could run. Maybe they could even help their Eliza and her family.

She shook that thought out of her head. Although it was tempting to have someone they trusted, even someone that Vell was comfortable with, they were not trained in any shape or form. And besides, being close to Vell would always endanger their lives.

"Though it would be nice for Vell to have some he could mate with," she said wistfully. She laughed at herself when she realized what she had just said. *Elliana is a sweet girl, but she deserves a stable future.*

Keiara's thoughts were all over the place. Hope and worry mingled to create threads of what-ifs that muddle her usually-clear soldier mind. This was obviously something that had been the result of peace and too much time. It was easy during the war. Pack up your things and bail before the horrors came, Scourge or otherwise. If this choice had come up during the war, she and Vell would have already been riding away. But...

Keiara rubbed her temples. They ached. She did not know if it was because of her thoughts or the lack of sleep.

Where was I?

The harder she thought, the foggier her mind seemed to be. She stood up and stretched. She drowned the rest of her drink and went to make more. She paced around with the hot cup in hand going over the facts again.

The mercenaries were going to the Wall. The Wall held back the Scourge, but it was not a certainty. If anything happened, she wanted to be as far away as possible. But she was worried about the people, her friends and neighbors and…

Keiara sighed. The bonds she had made over the years were making it difficult for her to make a decision.

She shook her head and paced some more.

Vell.

If she ran away with Vell, she would not be able explain why if she ended up returning. If she did not return, she would have to remake their lives again. If nothing happened and did not return, then she would be restarting their lives for nothing. And if something did happen, she would have basically abandoned almost everything she had come to care for in the past decade.

The best way to make sure nothing happened was to go and help at the Wall. Despite the guild being full of veterans, very few actually spent a lot of time fighting the Scourge directly. From the way they told their tales, it seemed that most who had experience fighting the Scourge had only been in a few scuffles with them; very few had any major confrontation, and if they did, that was their only experience. Keiara on the other hand experienced the Scourge almost non-stop. It was an event, a party even, if they did not fight the Scourge for more than two days at a time. Nights were the worst.

If they were to have a real chance of surviving a Scourge attack, it would be with her standing with her guildmates. It would also be the best chance to contain it.

But she could not leave Vell alone. Vell could not even remember the times they were on the run except in nightmares. How would he defend himself from the Scourge? Sure, he's a great fighter, but that's not all there is to it. Too many great fighters and armies of great fighters were easily overwhelmed by the Scourge. And no, Vell could not remember his experiences, or how he had fought. She needed to be with him. She had no idea how he would turn out if she could not be with him. If she…

Keiara shivered at the thought. Her eyes watered. She sucked in air deeply through her nose, hoping to plug the tears from falling and the thought from forming in her mind.

Her mind went back to the conversation she had with Eliza at dinner. She had mentioned that maybe Keiara coddled the boy a bit too much. He had grown, but he was still a young, little boy in Keiara's mind. And Keiara had hard time disputing that. What really shocked her was when Vell said he wanted to be a mercenary. How was she supposed to keep him safe when he wanted to do a job that was dangerous? As a highly-skilled mercenary, Keiara made it look easy, but she knew the truth – survival. She needed to survive so she could come home. Even the missions that were supposed to be difficult were often not much harder than the training she had gone through when she was younger. And needless to say, it did not even come close to the horrors she had to face during the war.

She finished her drink and went to wash up.

Maybe... maybe I can leave him here with Eliza and her family. Even if I'm gone, he will at least have someone that he can trust.

It was an unsatisfactory conclusion, but Keiara was beyond tired. She still had not quite recovered from her last mission.

She walked upstairs and to her room, but a voice called her.

"Mommy?" the voice said. "Mommy?"

When Keiara opened the door to Vell's bedroom, the soft cries for her were accompanied by soft sobs and a gentle stream of tears.

Keiara sat on his bed and held him gently. His calls for her softened as he mumbled undecipherable words before fading back into heavy breathing.

She sat there for a long while, her hand on his head and holding his other hand. Her vision blurred as the tears she had so easily held in earlier pooled in her eyes and down her cheeks.

She patted his head softly as she said, her voice wavering, "Sssh, mommy's here."

"Vell, pack up your gear," Keiara said. "We need to go."

"Go where?" Vell asked. "We're not training today?"

It had been a few days since Keiara came home from her previous mission. There were smaller contracts around town that she could've taken to fill her time, but she had turned those down. She had wanted to spend more time at home with Vell, and Vell was very happy that she did.

Keiara did not answer Vell's question. They were going to do something that could be considered training, but not the training that Vell was referring to.

"Just pack up your training gear and let's go," she said.

Vell started to whine.

"Stop, Vell," Keiara said. "Boys your age don't whine like that."

"Okay," he said. Then he gave her a big hug – the type that a little boy would give his mommy.

"And people your age do not give hugs like this," she said with a smile. She spoke the truth, but she did not hate that he still hugged her like that.

"People my age don't know or do a lot of things I do," Vell said, still hugging his mother, "and that doesn't bother me."

Keiara smiled and then patted his head. "Okay, okay, but at least act like you're older in public. You can't act like a little boy forever."

"But I'll always be your little boy," he said with a smile.

All Keiara could do was sigh. There was no winning this argument. She just hugged him tighter for a long moment before releasing him and making him pack his gear.

Vell still was not able to guess what they were doing by the time they reached their destination. All his guesses were close, but still off the mark. All Keiara would say is that it was a surprise.

She knew Vell wanted to whine, but he didn't. To be fair, he usually was stoic when in public and around other people, however he sometimes did forget to control himself.

But when they walked through the doors, Vell could not help but forget to control his emotions.

"Wow," he exclaimed. It had been a long time since he was surprised enough for the emotion to bleed through on his face. "There is a lot more people here in the guild than usual."

Before Keiara could respond, a familiar voice greeted them.

"Keiara!" said the guildmaster. "I thought you weren't going to join us today."

"I see that it didn't stop you from going forward," she said, "as you implied it would." Her eyes narrowed at the guildmaster in mock accusation.

Whether the guildmaster was actually nervous or just a great actor, he visibly looked unsettled under Keiara's glaring eyes. "W-Well, I had to do something," he stammered. "Wouldn't want a riot over missing such an opportunity."

Keiara visibly relaxed, but on the inside she still felt unsure of her decision. But action was better than inaction.

"I assume Vell's here to help with the evaluation?" the guildmaster asked.

"You could say that," Keiara replied. "I thought it would be interesting for him to see how the government soldiers fought."

Vell gave the guildmaster a rare genuine smile.

The guildmaster smiled back awkwardly before excusing himself and walking away.

Keiara chuckled at the exchange.

After a few rounds of chatting and catching-up with her fellow colleagues, a call rang out announcing that the evaluations were going to begin. The crowd took their time to move from the main area of the guildhall to the back of the building where an arena was set.

The arena was not large in relevance to other arenas in the world, but for a town this size where the guild was usually restricted to members, the arena was incredibly large. Keiara never understood why the arena was built to be so big. Sure it gave plenty of room for individual sparring matches and training regimens, but even if the entire guild and their families sat in the arena seats, it would still look like an unpopular event on account of the large number of empty seats left.

Vell rushed to get a front-row seat. He did not want to miss the action. Keiara took her time knowing there would be plenty of room. She enjoyed watching Vell being excited about something, even if it was a fight.

A small delegation of government officials, along with their retinue, sat in an area reserved for VIPs. The guildmaster and some others joined them.

In the ring, several government soldiers readied themselves. Most looked older and seemed to be trainers or at least experienced. Some could've been veterans, but most veterans never stayed with the government forces if they could help it. There were a handful of soldiers who looked younger, but they definitely did not look like young recruits who needed training.

The first set of mercenaries to be evaluated lined up inside the arena. They did not look as sharp as the soldiers, but they did not need to. A few of the soldiers came out and were designated a competitor from the line of mercenaries.

Each fight was individual. Nothing fancy. It was, after all, just an evaluation match – not a real sparring match.

The first were standard fare, as they should be. However, the guildmaster was eager to impress, and it was hard to see if the delegation was impressed. It was difficult to overcome the preconceptions both sides had of each other: one side, useless and a waste of space; the other side, money hungry and loyal-less, blood-thirsty showmen.

Tilian was called up next. He, of course, put on a show. The skill he demonstrated more than showed his aptitude in combat, but for someone who was more accustomed to the battlefield than showy tournaments, the light sparring was not enough to truly demonstrate his skills.

Still, the crowd seemed to love it, and so did members of the delegation. However, Keiara could tell that not all of them were impressed. The guildmaster's nervous posture showed that he had taken note of the discontent as well. He glanced over in Keiara's direction and their eyes met. Keiara gave a slight nod and he understood.

"Alright ladies and gentlemen," he said in a loud voice, "next up, we have another one of our most experienced veterans – the most experienced, in fact." With flourish, he pointed at Keiara. She put on her charm and smiled at everyone.

"Considering the type of contract, I have decided not to fight," Keiara announced. The guildmaster almost had a heart attack right next to his possible patrons. The sight made it hard for her to suppress the smirk that was forming. However, the statement had the desired effect on the unimpressed members of the delegation; a raised eyebrow, indicating a bit of amusement and, more importantly, interest. Some of the government soldiers on the other hand snickered at the thought of a delicate looking woman as the guild's most experienced veteran, though her comrades knew better. In any case, she had everyone's attention.

After the dramatic pause to survey the crowd, she continued. "Since it is a training mission," Keiara said, "I have decided to let my protégé fight in my stead."

She turned to Vell, but he had not reacted to the words. He seemed lost in his own world as he stared into the arena, waiting for the next fight.

"Surprise, Vell," she said softly. Vell looked at her and blinked.

"First a woman, than a boy?" a soldier in the arena guffawed. He could not keep his incredulousness to himself any longer. "This is waste of time."

Keiara smiled.

"Vell, you're going to spar with him," she said loud enough for everyone in the arena to hear.

The soldier's face grimaced. He almost yelled something before Vell cut him off.

"Okay, but he doesn't want to waste time so I'll have to finish it quickly. If I do, can I spar with the rest?"

The soldier's face turned crimson red. "W-Who do..." he started to yell, but was cut off again.

"I don't know, Vell, you might hurt him if you try to finish it too fast," Keiara said. She made sure that her voice carried through the silent arena. "Go to the arena and prepare," she said to Vell over the loud laughter that erupted.

Vell did not look too happy. *You're too greedy sometimes, Vell,* she scoffed in amusement. *I guess it could be worse.*

When Vell entered the arena he prepared himself calmly, like any other sparring match. To the angry soldier that waited, it seemed like Vell was taking his sweet time.

"Come on, boy," the soldier goaded, "let's get this over with so we can get on to better things."

"You don't like sparring?" Vell asked the soldier without looking up from his preparations.

The soldier gritted his teeth. "I don't like wasting my time with little boys." It looked like he wanted to say something else, but Vell cut him off again.

"Okay, I understand," he said as he faced and squared up to his opponent.

Keiara chose this moment to stoke the fire.

"Remember, Vell, don't hurt him too badly," she yelled.

"Okay, mom," he yelled back. This solicited another round of laughter and yells of encouragement for Vell.

It was no longer a mere evaluation to the soldier. He needed to prove his worth.

Like a true, foolish government soldier.

He roared as he ran at Vell. The soldier had completely given up his defenses and shredded all trace of tactics. It was pure rage and instinct – the worst type of person to spar with Vell.

The soldier, while not as big as Tilian, still looked massive compared to Vell. The bulk of his frame was muscle covered in a thick layer of fat. Intimidation probably came easy to someone like him.

He was definitely the worst type of opponent for Vell to spar against.

Keiara tried to shout a warning, but it was too late.

The soldier's bulk of rage bore down on Vell as he stood his ground. But at almost the last instant, Vell's sword blinked into another position as he fluidly side-stepped the soldier. The resulting *CRACK* echoed endlessly across the whole arena.

Keiara noticed Vell's eyes at the moment where they changed its intensity from focused to stoic. Her mind mentally clicked its tongue.

Vell relaxed his stance. He would usually stay in position to put up his guard even if the opponent seemed to be down for the count. But Vell did not hold his stance. After a short moment, he sheathed his sword.

The soldier had been knocked back by the blow. The spectators probably questioned their eyes and memories as to whether the soldier really flew back. Even if he did not, he was lying far away from where Vell had stood.

From Keiara's viewpoint, she could not see if the training blade had actually cut into the soldiers flesh; even a dull cleaver can cut meat. She could tell, however, that the chest piece had shattered around the stomach area. Even though Vell had not hit the soldier's chest, the blow to the gut could still have done some major damage.

"Don't worry, mom," Vell yelled up from the arena. Keiara turned to look at her son. She realized then that her facial expression displayed the look of shock. She tried very hard to relax, but it was made infinitely easier by what Vell said next. "I didn't kill him."

As if to answer, a groan came from the soldier. One of his teammates was kneeling next to him to check if he was still alive, and he lifted his hand in a sign that confirmed what Vell and the groan had said: he was still alive.

The arena was quiet for a long time, with the hissing sound of sporadic whispers carrying further than they normally would. The whispers gained traction and soon become murmurs of commentary and awe. Someone started clapping, and others slowly joined in. Scattered cheers and whistles added to the mix before it all amplified in concert to form a torrent of accolades. Even members of the delegation who had not been impressed before had stood up and joined in with a dignified form of clapping. The fight had given the people what they wanted. A show.

But things had not gone entirely in the direction that Keiara had wanted. *Maybe I shouldn't have goaded the soldier so much.* It had been a habit she picked up on the battlefield. One of the sad things about the war was that they often had to fight other people even as they were running from the Scourge. She had learnt that emotions could cloud someone's mind, and she often used it to her advantage. Another tactic was to effectively take down an opponent so there is no wastage of strength. A lot of battles came down to stamina. And taking down that first opponent in a way that showed total domination would often rattle the mindset of the remaining opponents. Keiara's trainers had called that 'Psy Ops' or psychological warfare. There were other elements to it, but turning the mind of the enemy against themselves was a tool she employed often.

Vell had taken advantage of the uncontrollable rage of the soldier and then employed the other tactics. Whether he did so knowingly or through instinct was a different story. Unfortunately it could be confused as a display of showmanship, not tactics or proper training.

And it seemed that someone had noticed.

"I'm not sure that display shows anything about training," a gruff member of the delegation said. He had timed the words to fit into a lull in the noise of the spectators. He did not need to shout to be heard. "But that is more our fault than the boy's," he said.

The man looked almost weary, but that would've been a mistake. His gruffness in both countenance and voice, mixed with the weary look of a man bored with theatrics masquerading as combat, was indicative of experience on the battlefield or at least some sort of actual warfare. The man stood up and left his seat. The guildmaster stumbled over his robe and over his words as he tried to go after the gruff man, but the guildmaster was waved off. The other members of the delegation looked at the gruff man's back as he departed.

It looked like it was over.

Keiara was conflicted by the turn of events. On one hand, she had helped put an end to the mission evaluation and let down her guild. On the other hand, she would not have to deal with the Wall and would not have to leave Vell alone.

But the turn of events had not finished turning.

The gruff man reappeared in the arena in garb and gear more suited for a fight. His weariness seemed to have morphed into sharpness as he stretched his body.

After he had limbered up, the man turned to look up at Keiara who was still in the stands.

"Ms. Keiara, if you don't mind, I would love a chance to spar with your protégé."

Keiara nodded.

The man turned to Vell. "I hope you do not mind humoring an old soldier like myself," he said with a respectful bow. "But please don't be in such a rush to end our match," he continued with a grin.

Vell nodded apologetically. "Sorry. I felt it was safer, for the both of us, if I ended the match quickly."

The man took a sword and took his stance against Vell. He smiled knowingly. "He did say he did not want to waste time with little boys."

Vell took his stance as well.

The match had started.

Both fighters kept their distance from each other. Occasionally they would move sideways with the other mirroring the movement, which lead to them circling each other. Keiara was not sure if the gruff soldier was trying to avoid the mistake the previous soldier made by charging in, or if he was just gauging Vell.

The first few moments felt like forever.

But then, in a flash, Vell went in. The gruff man, though he had been waiting, let down his guard for a split second. Vell had caught it and charged in.

The gruff man barely countered. It was a good counter by any measure, clearly a sign of real battle experience, however he had never seen Vell's real fighting style before. As soon as he parried and countered, Vell was gone.

In the eyes of the opponent on the ground, it would've seemed like Vell had vanished. The controlled but slightly frantic movements the gruff man's head made were a clear sign of searching for his opponent. Unfortunately for him, Vell did not move like a normal solider would have. He had already slid behind the soldier and across to the opposite side of where he had attacked.

The soldier spun around in his search, and saw Vell just in time to block again. This time, Vell used a controlled backwards tumble to gain some distance. This also bought the soldier a moment to catch his breath and reorient himself.

Vell recovered deftly and got into his stance. The difference this time was that he swayed his body back and forth, like a serpent, in order to confuse the enemy even more. It might not work if used by normal soldiers, but anyone who had just experienced Vell's fighting style would now, unconsciously, be hyper aware of any slight movements. The swaying movement could lull one into a state of hypnosis, or, in this case, cause the opponent to subtly flinch at each movement, wearing down their awareness.

The soldier charged forward, denying Vell another chance to strike first. Vell parried – hard – and caused the soldier to stumble back. Then Vell used the counter momentum to put himself into a spin and strike on the opposite end. The soldier half-stumbled and half-blocked Vell's sword as he fell down.

He rolled away in a much less elegant fashion than Vell had done earlier and avoided Vell's next strike, this time from above. The soldier was still on his back when another strike landed. This time, the solder had held the flat of the blade with his other hand and pushed upward strongly against Vell's strike in an attempt to destabilize Vell long enough for the soldier to get back up.

But that didn't work so well.

Vell had jumped into the strike, and when pushed back, had used the momentum to flip backwards and back into a low-standing stance.

The soldier quickly stood back up and readied his stance, but then realized that Vell had already been in his own stance, waiting for the soldier to get up. The surprise was displayed obviously on his face

He clicked his tongue. It seemed like he needed more practice and training as well. A smile broke out across his face as he let down his stance and admitted defeat.

"I know when I need to stop," he said as he took off his helmet. "I don't need to be knocked out and on my back to know that."

Vell relaxed.

Overall, it was still a short match. This time though, Vell did not complain.

The evaluation continued after that, but the general consensus was that the job was theirs and this was more about individual evaluation. The soldiers took their roles more seriously, as well as the rest of the mercenaries.

As expected, Keiara did not have to personally spar after Vell's matches. The delegation was very clear that they wanted Keiara and her son to join. However, Vell would not be there as an official mercenary. He would, instead, be there as a teaching assistant – or a sort of visual aid of the benefits of training. Nothing would motivate a soldier to take training seriously than a kid who clearly outclassed them.

Preparations were still being made as the day for departure quickly approached. The contract was a long one, with a clause for extension, and required the mercenaries to have affairs settled for an extended period of time. Most were used to it and already had some sort of arrangement in place with just the details to be hammered out.

For Keiara and Vell, the arrangements were less complex than usual: only the house needed a watchful eye this time. Ms. Eliza and her family were more than happy to help.

The night before the departure, with most of the major arrangements made, Keiara found herself in her room still packing. She kept thinking of things to bring and things she no longer wanted to bring, bustling from here to there. But she knew the real reason for her discomfort, the real reason she felt like she was missing something.

Finally, she gave in.

She approached an innocuous part of the room's floor and knelt down. After a bit of twiddling and finessing, she lifted a part of the floor out of its position. It had been years since she had even bothered to check the secret compartment.

Nothing was out of place. In it still laid her armor and gear from her time on the run. During the war, while on the run, the engravings and markings on her armor were obscured in an effort to conceal their origins. However, over time, she had taken the effort to restore them, as well as she could, to their original state. She had hoped that she would never need her armor again. But she felt uneasy about this trip. Anything to do with the Scourge made her uneasy. She would've felt better if she brought all her gear with her, just in case. However, she had managed to keep her past a secret all these years. She trusted some of the people around her enough to reveal bits and pieces, but never all of it and definitely never the important parts. But taking her armor, and certainly wearing her armor, would solicit too many questions that cannot be answered in any way that would not involve problems.

She moved to put the floor cover back over her secret compartment. But something made her pause. No matter how hard she tried, she could not move to put it back. Eventually she gave up with a sigh and set the floor cover back off to the side. She then lightly rummaged through the compartment, half-heartedly, hoping to calm her anxiousness.

Her hand settled on a satchel. She knew what was in it. She picked it up and checked to see if things were still as they were. They were. She also spotted a dagger that could work and would be inconspicuous enough not to raise any questions. She carefully positioned it in the satchel and seemed satisfied with her choice.

She moved to put the floor cover back, but something else caught her eye. Something that she had missed but now could not take her eyes off of. Memories flooded her mind as she picked it up and stared at it.

"I haven't seen you since..." She could not remember when she last saw it, but the necklace, or trinket, had been with her as far back as she could remember. It was a memento given to her by her parents or guardians, a relic from the ancient past. The symbol it emulated in a shiny, silver-ish metal had been the basis of much of the family crests of her people, especially of those in the old, elite families. A simple, rectangular shape in the middle of the symbol shot up towards the sky. It was flanked on either side by curved but angular wing-like shapes. It was inlaid atop of a tear-shaped background, and the symbol was further inlaid on a sort of material that was not quite stone but not quite metal. She had heard that the symbol represented a flying bird, but others had said it represented the name of their people in the old language. Whatever it may have been, it was important to her people and showed up everywhere in their designs. From their family crests, to even their military insignias, the symbol was somehow a basis of so many of their designs.

And now, almost everyone that knew anything about the symbol had disappeared. Even the little that she knew would disappear completely. Vell had seen the symbol, but he was so young that it was impossible for him to have even thought to question the origins of the symbol. And Keiara knew that the meaning of the symbol would disappear in the folds of history if she did not pass it on.

She struggled with it. Her people had disappeared from existence; will she let them disappear from history as well? Can she pass it on? Will it trigger something in Vell's mind that would bring the past back to him – or his trauma?

"Vell," she called out.

He arrived almost immediately. He still looked excited. She smiled.

"Have you finished packing?" she asked.

"Almost, just making sure I have everything," he said.

She held out the necklace for Vell.

"What's that?" he asked as he took it and examined it. "It…" he paused. Anxiousness crept up the back of Keiara's mind. "…looks familiar."

He continued to toy with it as if he expected his memories to hold the answer to where he had seen it before.

"The symbol was on my armor and weapons," she offered.

His face brightened. "Oh yeah, from the time we were running," he said. He then looked over Keiara's shoulder and spotted the armor sitting in the secret compartment. "We used to hide it, but it looks like you've restored your armor to its original look," he said.

"We should still keep it to ourselves," she said, "but it is the proud symbol of our families and our people."

Keiara looked at Vell's face intently.

"Do you remember our time on the run?" she asked tepidly.

Vell shook his head. "I remember bits and pieces, but I don't really want to remember more than that," he said.

A proper mother would've encouraged him to face his fears so that he can get passed them and grow, but Keiara had her own fears and it hurt every time she thought of what she would have to do to overcome them.

"Are you okay?" Vell asked his mother.

"I'm fine," she smiled as she mentally shook her mind to get rid of the tendrils of dark thoughts.

Vell handed back the necklace, but Keiara put her hands over his and helped him clasp it again. "It's for you," she said.

"Really?" he said. "Why are you giving this to me now?"

She did not really have an answer. Tears started to well up in her eyes as she looked down at the floor. She could not coax herself to look up at Vell.

"I-It's so you remember me, us, by," she stuttered. Her voice had betrayed what she had tried to hide.

"I don't want it," Vell said.

Keiara was shocked by what he said. She looked up, forcing the tears she held back to roll obviously down her cheeks. She rubbed her eyes and looked at Vell again. His face was serious.

"If you give this to me so that I can remember you, then you are thinking something might happen during the mission," he said.

The intelligence in the thought disoriented Keiara.

"In that case, I don't want it," he said, putting the necklace in his mother's lap. "I don't want you to use it as an excuse to give up easily. I would rather have you than a thought of you."

Keiara couldn't help but get up and embrace Vell. She let out a soft sob. Vell had hit the matter right on the head.

Vell held her too. After a moment, Vell softly whispered into her ear, "I love you, mommy..."

Keiara could not hear the rest as she let go the torrent of her tears.

She did not know how long it went on before she could bring herself back under her normal control. Vell patiently waited throughout, holding her firmly and never letting up. In such a short time, it had felt like he had grown up, and now Keiara had trouble letting him go. This boy that was not related to her by blood, this boy who was not her real son, this boy that was not even her assigned charge, this boy... she could not let go of.

But she had to.

"It's for you, to celebrate you growing up to a young man," she said as she let go of the embrace and smiled at the boy. "We go on your first mission tomorrow," she said. "You may not be an official mercenary, but it is still a mission you're getting paid for."

Vell smiled. His excitement had returned.

It seemed that Keiara had convinced him. But she still needed to convince herself.

"Let's finish packing and getting ready so we can sleep enough for the trip," she said.

Vell nodded. He took the necklace, and with Keiara's help, he put it on. He hid the trinket under his tunic, remembering that he needed to hide his past.

They bid their goodnights to each other and proceeded to finish packing and preparing.

And as Keiara lay in bed, just before the tiredness overcame her thoughts, it said, *Will he be okay without me?*

5

Elliana had dreaded this day.

When she heard the news, her heart sank. She did not even know what to call the turmoil of feelings that refused to give her peace. Was it because of the confusing feelings she had for Vell? Or was it the feeling of familiarity that came with the ebb and flow of routine? Or was it fear of the unknown? She could not quite figure it out.

It was only recently that she had been able to find a word that fit close enough to use: dread.

Even then, it was not a perfect way to describe her feelings. It felt like her feelings were more complicated than other people, and that language could not neatly describe it in the simple package of a word.

That morning, even as the entire town was abuzz with excitement, Elliana did not know what to do with her dread.

She moved from task to task, to figuring out what to do next, then to the next task so she could keep her mind off of it. Time would pass, and then she could deal with what would happen then. At the moment, she did not want to think about it. She did not know what to do and was putting it off as much as she could.

But eventually Elliana found herself in the center of town with her family, and almost everyone in the town who could spare a moment, to see their friends, families, and neighbors off. The convoy for both the mercenaries and members of the government delegation stretched from the edge of town all the way to the guild hall, through the town center. Almost the entire town had played some part in the expedition.

It was amazing how this town, small and quaint just a decade ago, had grown so much with businesses that supported the mercenaries and, in turn, the business that the mercenaries brought into town. That cycle had helped bring prosperity to the town, but yet the town remained close-knit. Everyone was friendly and neighbors helped each other. Sure there were some exceptions, but nothing like the isolation and general disregard found in the bigger cities that benefitted from mercenaries. It wasn't the selfish type where winner takes all.

Elliana sighed. At least that's what she heard. She had never left town. To her, the guildhall was still the most amazing tourist attraction she had seen. And to these brave people who dared to take the chance to travel out of the comfort of their homes to the unknown, it was just a small part of the world.

"Are you okay, Elliana?" her mother asked.

Elliana looked at her mother and rubbed away the bit of moisture that had unexpectedly gathered in her eyes. She nodded at her mother in response, but her mother did not look convinced.

"Hello Eliza, Petr," a voice called. It was Ms. Keiara. She dismounted her horse and walked towards them. Elliana strained to look behind Ms. Keiara for sings of Vell, but did not see any.

"Are you ready for the big adventure?" Elliana's father, Petr, asked.

"I'm not sure," she said with a smirk. "Releasing Vell into the wild is a big adventure for everyone. I'm more concerned that the world is not ready for him yet."

Elliana's parents laughed. She joined in as well, but she was not sure what was so funny.

"Well, I've heard your concerns, but hopefully everything will be okay," Elliana's mother offered.

Ms. Keiara nodded in response.

"Remember, if there is an outbreak, take everyone and run," Ms. Keiara said.

This scared Elliana a little. *What did she mean by 'outbreak'?*

"Are you ready, Vell," Elliana's father said.

Elliana looked up and saw Vell approaching. He had a small bag slung over his shoulder, and his sword and shield on his back. The gear looked different than his usual training gear – more solid and… real.

"A-Are you…" Elliana stopped herself when she realized she was about to ask the same question her father just asked.

Vell looked directly at her, and nodded. He looked like his usual expressionless self, but there was something different. It looked like there was a hint of some emotion that he was actively hiding.

Elliana took a deep breath and let it out again. She smiled, hiding her own emotions, and asked, "Are you excited?"

He smiled slightly. It seemed like he was trying very hard to hold back. "Yes," he managed to say.

Elliana felt conflicted.

She smiled back. "I hope you have fun exploring the world," she said.

"Thanks."

"Where are your friends, Elliana," Ms. Keiara asked.

"Oh…" Elliana said, thinking. "Well, Lucinda is helping with the family business, loading up the supplies and whatnot." She paused. She was not sure how to explain Tatiana's whereabouts.

Just then, a massive shadow towered over Elliana. "And I told my family to stay home," a voice with a strong accent said.

"As expected," Ms. Keiara replied to the voice. "You did not want to cry in front of everyone."

"Aye," Mr. Tilian replied. "What's the use for all of us to be sobbing in public like wee babies? That doesn't show well in my line of work."

They laughed.

It was weird to hear his accent, because Tatiana did not speak like them. She only did so when she was making fun of her brothers or her father. It was hilarious to watch because she had to exaggerate her face to get the words to sound right. The shock of red hair tossing about as she contorted her face to say the words added comedic flair.

"Well, are you all ready to go?" Mr. Tilian said.

"Not quite," Ms. Keiara said. "Let us bid our farewells."

"Alright," Mr. Tilian said with a nod, "we'll move out soon." He turned around and proceeded to walk away, but he stopped in mid stride – leg half lifted off the ground when he heard a simple word called from behind the crowd.

"Da?"

It was Tatiana.

And she did not look like herself.

Mr. Tilian literally froze for a long moment before he put his foot down and turned to face his daughter. You could almost hear the creaking his joints made as his body stuttered in its attempt to face Tatiana.

"Tati?" he said.

Tatiana hated that nickname.

But she pushed her way past the crowd and even her friend's family to rush to her father, sobbing. She kept on muttering and sniffing and sobbing, so nothing that came out of her mouth made sense.

I guess Tatiana loves her father after all, Elliana thought. She realized her mouth hung open and quickly closed it.

"Why do you a-always have to do something dangerous," Tatiana whined. "Why can't you do something normal and stay in town?"

Mr. Tilian did not offer an answer. He just held his blubbering daughter tightly as his own tears ran down his cheeks.

Tatiana hit him in the side with her fist. It wasn't meant to hurt, but the sound made it feel like it did.

"You know this is how I provide for you and the family, Tatiana," Mr. Tilian said.

Tatiana hit him again. "But can't you farm or be a maker or something? Why do you have to do something so dangerous," she yelled into Mr. Tilian, his body muffling the pain. She hit him again for good measure.

Mr. Tilian just smiled. "I don't think I'm cut out to be a farmer or a maker," he said. "I'm good at breaking things though, and too many people depend on me."

Tatiana continued to sob, but the intensity had diminished.

She looked up at her 'Da' and said something softly. Elliana could not hear what Tatiana said, but she could guess. Tatiana then reached into her pants pocket and took out a small wooden token. She had made it in school after she finished her other work. Elliana had remembered that it didn't look great, and Lucinda made fun of her for it. But now it looked much better and had more polish than before. Elliana felt bad when she realized that Tatiana had made that for her dad.

Mr. Tilian took the offered token from Tatiana and examined it carefully. Tears started streaming down his face again. He then suddenly picked up Tatiana in a big bear hug. "I told your ma and your brothers not to see me off," he said. "Now look at my face! Is this a face that can lead soldiers?"

"Who cares!" Tatiana yelled. "I had to hide from Lucinda to see you, you dumb bag of muscle. Now let me down!"

Despite her protest, it looked like neither of them had the intention to let go.

Finally, Mr. Tilian let go of his daughter. She crumpled into a mess as soon as her feet hit the ground. She still sobbed softly, but had seemed to calm down.

She turned to Elliana. Her face looked terrible. She mouthed silently to Elliana, *Don't you dare tell Luci.*

Elliana just waved back. She could not hide the smile she had, and Tatiana obviously did not like it.

Mr. Tilian had calmed down as well. He announced to the rest, "Alright, get your farewells out of the way so we can move out." His voice cracked at the last word. The crowd was quietly amused, but they already knew Mr. Tilian was a passionate man.

"Vell, it's time to go," Ms. Keiara said. "Are you ready?"

"No."

"Okay," Ms. Keiara said. "Let's finish up, shall we?"

Vell nodded.

Ms. Keiara bid farewell to Elliana's parents and thanked them for helping her out again. They talked about Vell and how it must have been exciting for him to go on his first mission. Vell then thanked Elliana's parents and even gave them a quick hug.

"Be good," Elliana's father said.

"I'll be more than good, I'll be great," Vell quipped.

Elliana held out her hand when Vell walked to her. "Be careful," she said. "And come home soon."

Vell took her hand. She expected a simple handshake, but instead she found herself pulled into Vell's arms. He hugged her tightly. The moment seemed to last forever for Elliana. She did not know what to do.

"Thank you," Vell whispered into Elliana's ear.

Elliana was flustered. She could feel the intense heat radiate from her body. She felt like she had a fever, like her body was on fire. The hottest part of that fire was where her body was in contact with Vell.

She wanted to pull away. She did not want Vell to feel the heat too. But by the time she came to her senses, Vell had already let go and walked to one of the transport wagons preparing for departure.

Her eyes focused on Vell as he climbed into the wagon. His eyes met hers as he reached the top of the steps. He paused as he looked at her, and smiled.

All Elliana could muster, with every force of her being, was a wave. Vell waved back.

Then he was gone.

6

It was only a few days ride to the fort, but Wilhelm's body ached. A less reasonable person could blame the road, the horse, the weather, or even the built-up fatigue from travelling all over the country, but Wilhelm knew that his body was just tired of this life. He wanted to retire.

He wasn't old when compared to the elders of the world or even some of the mercenaries he's come across over the years. But he was considered old – ancient even – by government army standards. Most joined to get a start in the world, either money, experience or a free ride to experience the world. Once they gained what they needed, they moved on. Becoming a mercenary was an option for most foot soldiers, travelling merchants or makers for those trained in support roles, even leadership positions in different outposts or towns. To most, the government forces were a stepping stone.

But considering the war had decimated the forces so badly, it was a wonder that there were people who were still desperate enough to join the army. Government forces were the first line of defense against the Scourge, or more accurately, the first sacrifice. The civilians were not equipped to fight, so instead sacrificed everything they could to support the war effort. Both sides felt that the other had not done enough. Eventually tensions rose up between civilians and the soldiers. Both required help, but neither side was willing to give – civilians saw the soldiers as incompetent parasites ready to run at a moment's notice, and the soldiers saw the civilians as ungrateful burdens who forced heroic men and women to die so that the civilians could run. And those sentiments turned into a self-fulfilling prophesy.

Now there was a generation of inexperienced soldiers who had not even laid eyes on the Scourge before, let alone fought them. Even Wilhelm himself had only seen the Scourge from a distance; which is probably why he had lived while others had not. To this day, he regretted not leaving his post to help those on the frontlines – too many good people died that day – but he had heard of too many heroes that sacrificed themselves while abandoning tactics and defenses. Brave but stupid. Those acts often crumbled resolves more than steel them.

But that left an army with very little experience, and over the past ten years, it had caused the effectiveness and professionalism of the army to deteriorate to an embarrassing level. Thankfully, the excess of mercenaries to help keep things under control, and the focus of the civilians on trying to rebuild their lives, had caused the masses to shift their attention away from how bad things had become. On the surface, the government forces were simply living up to their reputation.

After ten years of quiet, the politicians and elites wanted to put their useless standing army to good use. The army that once had trouble retaining numbers now was considered a safe-haven for people to feed off of the government while they trained to do other things. Some politician who fancied themselves a crafty tactician may have suggested that the government use their useless army to take back the territory lost to the Scourge. If the Scourge had disappeared, then they would gain back territory and open up more convenient trade routes again. If the Scourge had not disappeared, the numbers of the soldiers would diminish.

Of course, the elites never thought of the risk that they would put themselves in if a breach in the Wall was not sealed in time. And the likelihood of that happening was high with forces as ill-prepared as the current crop of soldiers. Even an army made of hardened veterans of previous wars could not hold their ground against the Scourge. It was a disaster in the making.

Wilhelm clicked his tongue.

Thankfully, the ruling family had not blindly followed the advice of the elites. They had learnt lessons from the war. The lessons weren't great, but at least they had learnt something, unlike the foolish elite.

His Majesty, King Ainsley, had ordered his army to search for mercenaries and veterans willing to train his troops to raise their combat level without actual combat. This increased the survivability of the troops – lesser or slower soldiers would have a chance to grow instead of just dying on the battlefield with their first misstep. Even if there were hardly any exceptional soldiers, the whole would be stronger and attrition may be lower. On top of that, His Majesty sent out the Crown Princess, Princess Ainsley II, along with the best of the best of the capitol's reserve forces, to raise an army made of the very best of the country. The troops trained by the mercenaries would be integrated into the Princess' army and used to open the Wall. All this both stacked the odds in the government's favor and stacked the faith of the government and the population in the initiative. But it was still a risky move.

To minimize the risks, the part of the Wall they were going to use as a foothold was one far to the south. The hope was that the Scourge, if they could not be contained, would continue moving southward as they had during the war. This would spare the bulk of the cities to the east, including the capitol. It also helped that the foothold had a large fort on the populated side, and another, smaller fort on the side with the Scourge. Whether the fort on the Scourge side still existed was another story.

Hopefully the mercenaries will be able to hold back the Scourge if the army fails, Wilhelm thought. The mercenaries who trained the army would not be part of the expedition past the Wall. If they went in with the normal troops, then the soldiers would depend on them; the mercenaries may even claim it was their efforts that helped take back a portion of the wall, taking away the glory of the army.

Wilhelm shook his head at the thought. It was a stupid thing to fight for, glory, when the enemy did not care for it.

The more logically reason was to allow the mercenaries to act as a backstop in case of failures or massive losses. Wilhelm did not think the mercenaries would mind. It gave them a safe way to make money, almost like a bet that nothing would go wrong. But if things did go wrong, it would be money well spent.

However, as with most plans, this one didn't go off without a problem. Maybe Wilhelm had been picky, but his delegation could not find enough veterans and mercenaries that were satisfactory. Most of the mercenaries who were willing to work with the government forces tended to be showy. Sure, a lot of them were skilled, but they displayed too much ambition and selfishness to impart into soldiers. Wilhelm had almost given up and had been planning on adjusting the training for his troops, but then he decided to go to a little town much further south than he had expected. And his expectations were flipped upside down.

The little town was not little at all. It would not compare to the hub cities, but it was not the hamlet that people made it out to be. "A haven for veterans and mercenaries to retire," was what someone had said, bringing to mind a guild full of old soldiers gabbing about the good old days. To find that the guild was thriving and had a good mix of talent was surprising on its own. Finding that boy and his mother was astounding.

Wilhelm looked at his hand. It trembled as he remembered the power of the young boy. *Not even an actual mercenary and still he fought better than most he'd seen.* But there was something else – something deeper. It was as if he had the eyes of someone who had witnessed the ugly side of war up close, and he had the presence of someone who had been through and survived the ugly side of war. But how could a young boy, not even an official mercenary, have experienced war? Maybe he had passed through the border territories and gotten caught up in the skirmishes?

"...Captain? Captain?"

Wilhelm's mind snapped back to the present.

"Are you alright, Captain Wilhelm?" a rider asked.

"I'm fine," Wilhelm replied. "Just deep in thought." The long, monotonous ride had caused his mind to preoccupy itself with endless musings. He cleared his throat, and then said, "What do you need?"

"We're getting close to the fort," the rider said. "Where should we set up camp?"

The forces in tow were bigger than what the fort was capable of sheltering. However, over the years, what started as a support outpost for the fort had transformed into a bustling town capable of supporting the additional forces. In addition to that, the convoy had brought extra supplies with them and will continue to be supplied over the course of the contract. The real problem would be the sheer amount of space needed for the forces to sleep and train.

"There is a large area near the fort and Wall that will be suitable for camp," Wilhelm said.

The rider did not look sure. "Near the Wall, sir?"

Wilhelm sighed. The rider visibly back down.

"We're not camping right in front of the gate, soldier," Wilhelm said. "The fort won't allow it. They need that space to mount a proper defense in case of a breach."

He turned to the rider and used his hands to explain what was meant by next to the fort. "We will be camping off to the side of the fort."

"S-Sorry for doubting you, sir," the rider said.

Wilhelm sighed again. That was not the lesson to take away from this exchange.

"It's okay to have some doubts, but you need to question if it is a doubt based on fear or laziness, or a doubt based on logic and experience," Wilhelm said, his voice less harsh than it had been a moment ago.

The rider nodded. "Thank you for taking the time to explain, Captain," he said.

Captain Wilhelm nodded back.

The troops had a long way to go in regards to training, but soldiers like that comforted Wilhelm. It was not a total lost cause.

But that depended on how the nobles and the aristocrats meddle with the affairs. Not *if*, but *how*, because they will meddle, regardless.

Wilhelm just hoped he could minimize the negative impact – militarily and politically.

The rest of the ride was spent in quiet contemplation. When the convoy arrived, the garrison from the fort directed them to the large open field to the right of the fortress, just outside of town. Several sections of tents and temporary buildings had already been erected, with signs of a lot more in progress. With the estimated numbers set to be around five to seven thousand soldiers and support personnel, Wilhelm noted that there was still a lot of work to do despite the progress.

The government forces had to make do with whatever they were given, but the mercenaries did not. Although the contract for the mission stipulated that accommodations and provisions were provided, the mercenaries could choose what to eat and where to sleep. And most chose the typical inns and accommodations offered in town.

Maybe that is what they are used to, Wilhelm thought. *Or maybe they did not want to be reminded of the soldier's life.*

Either way, it worked out. There was more than enough space for the currently stationed soldiers as well as the soldiers trickling in with the different delegation convoys. Wilhelm was one of the highest ranking officers, reporting only to the Commander and his assistant, the Sub-Commander. This afforded him better accommodations than the common foot soldier, a luxury he was happy to take advantage of. It really just meant he had a large room to himself; more room to show how little the government provided its troops.

I'll take more pay over excessive extras any day, Wilhelm thought.

Someone knocked on his door.

"Enter," Wilhelm said.

A soldier entered and said, "Captain Wilhelm, the Commander requires your attendance."

Requires, huh...

Wilhelm followed the soldier all the way to the fort. Then they proceeded upwards to a central room that was not far away from the important defensive structures and overlooks.

They walked to a large set of doors flanked by guards at attention with seating for those not deemed important enough to attend the meeting. Wilhelm sometimes wished he was not important enough to sit in on most meetings. However, he knew he had to be there just in case he needed to work the minds that considered the actions before it lead to chaos. No one would have to run from trouble if they did not run into it in the first place.

Wilhelm took a deep breath and steeled himself. It took just a moment, and then he looked up at the soldier who escorted him and nodded. The soldier signaled the guards and they let them in.

"Ah, there you are, Captain," an opulently dressed gentleman said. "It seems you finally found mercenaries worthy of your experienced eye?"

Wilhelm nodded. "Yes, Commander Lytton," he said. Wilhelm had noted the sarcasm in the commander's words, but did not sink himself to meet it.

"Good, good," the Commander said. The air he displayed made it seem that all was going well with his plans, when in fact he had somehow gotten himself appointed to this role on his way to bigger and greater things. This was a stepping stone for his ambitions, nothing more. He simply had to follow his instructions and babysit the forces until the main force arrived and the Princess took command. He did not have to think or anything except just sit and follow instructions blindly – a perfect job for him. "What about the support personnel?"

A weaselly man with a permanent, sly grin on his face answered with an overly-dramatic bow, "Commander, the artisans, makers and manual laborers have been given their assignments. High priority projects will be evaluated daily revolving around the needs of the training, then moving on to repairing and building of defensive projects with a special projects team working to get accommodations ready for the arrival of the Princess and the main forces."

The Commander clapped his hand and chortled with glee. "Excellent, Sub-Commander Mayne! Excellent!"

It took Wilhelm almost all his willpower to prevent himself from visibly reacting to the gross display of childish delight. Nothing wrong with being happy with one's work, but it seemed like the Commander did not understand how close they were to playing with fire – no, an inferno.

Wilhelm glanced over to the side and caught the eye of the fort commander. He smiled slightly. It seemed like Wilhelm hadn't hidden his reaction well enough.

The Commander vocalized his thought process. "Hmmm, the soldiers need to concentrate on training with the mercenaries. They need to be in tip-top shape before the Princess arrives. It would help with our standing when we head back to the capitol. That was our main mandate, so we will do it exceedingly well."

"Splendid strategy, Commander," the Sub-Commander said, rubbing his hands together.

They both laughed together as if they had just shared an inside joke.

The Commander paused long enough to look at both Wilhelm and the fort commander. "Anything you need, gentlemen, anything to make sure our troops are trained to the best... no, beyond their abilities!"

"Thank you, sir," both of the men answered in unison.

The Commander spread out his arms and slammed his palms onto the top of the strategy table. He looked intently at the map and the pieces on it. He searched and searched; for what, only he knew.

The weaselly man crept over to look at the map over the Commander's shoulder. He entertained the map for a while before he offered his advice. "Commander Lytton, it is a nice day out," he said. "We should walk the grounds and see what the troops on the ground need."

A wide grin appeared on the Commander's face. "Splendid idea, my friend! You're always full of wonderful advice."

With that, they both strode out and called an end to the meeting.

The other personnel in attendance looked around the room in confusion. Wilhelm just sighed and looked at the fort commander. The fort commander just responded with a raised eyebrow and a quizzical look on his face.

Wilhelm did not bother to hide his annoyance and pinched the bridge of his nose.

As long as those gloryhounds stay away from actual thinking, we should survive, Wilhelm thought. *Should.*

7

The morning sun had slowly risen and now sat high above the clouds. The gentle, cooling breeze that blew in the morning still contained a bit of the chill. Keiara stood at the finish line, waiting for the platoon to come up the hill. Very few obstacles blocked her line of sight; most of the surrounding area was fields full of tame grass. In an abstract sort of way, the terrain blended beautifully into solid colors that made the scenery look picturesque.

It had been a few weeks since they arrived at Fort Holden. Keiara had thought that the higher-ups would interfere in training, but they surprisingly gave the mercenaries a lot of freedom in how they structured the training. There were some incidences where the mercenaries were found to not be as competent in training, but mostly things progressed well. The troops had become more disciplined and organized. Their skills had improved significantly. But the most important improvement was to their tactics and teamwork, which had been next to non-existent. All of those improvements were made with ease – all they needed were experienced teachers willing to show them why they should do things a certain way, and not just shovel patterns and commands into their skulls. It convinced them that there was a reason for troops to do things a certain way, but it also allowed them the understanding to think in combat so that they could effectively use their training.

It also helped that they were embarrassed about being outclassed by the star object lesson, Vell.

But to be fair, the soldiers did not let that embarrassment turn into something evil. Instead, they used it as a challenge to overcome. If a normal boy could be this good, they could too.

Except Vell was not exactly normal. His lineage played a part, true, and so did his training when he was a little boy. But the real differentiator was the almost two years on the run, facing the Scourge almost every night. Imagine having the fight every night and somehow surviving. That person would be considered a veteran among veterans – a hero, even – but Vell never let on. Not because he was humble, not even because of his awkwardness; it was because he could not remember. Whether it was because of the trauma or because he was so young, or even a combination of the two, Keiara never really knew.

Keiara was just happy that the immense pressure and worry that Vell had – even the fear that he hid – had evaporated when he lost his memory.

Roaring screams pierced the air, and Keiara's senses sharpened, alert.

Just then, Vell came into view. He was in full combat gear with a survival pack on his back and weapons in place. His pace was quick, but his breathing and calmness made it seem like a simple morning jog. Even fully geared up, his body took the run in stride.

That put a smile on Keiara's face.

She heard the roaring screams again.

It did not come from Vell.

It came from behind him.

As Vell neared the finish line, far behind him a few soldiers came into view. They screamed and yelled again, motivating themselves to run forward against the protests of their tired bodies.

Keiara hadn't asked them to push themselves so hard. It was supposed to be at a good pace with full gear so they could build their stamina and tolerance for actual combat. Running in little-to-no gear was okay, but it would not be of much help when they have to both move and fight in combat. However, pushing so hard would wipe them out for the rest of the day and possibly the next day.

Still, many of the soldiers and even the less experienced mercenaries taking part in the training wanted to push themselves to get to the level of Vell. It was a worthwhile goal, especially when it contributed to increasing their survival rate on the battlefield.

Keiara laughed.

"Mom, are you okay?" Vell asked as he crossed the finish line.

Keiara just smiled.

"I was thinking of those guys working so hard to try and beat you," she said.

It was too bad that Vell wasn't improving his skills as well, Keiara left unsaid.

Vell had always been good, but his fighting style mirrored what Keiara and her partner had taught him based on their own styles they learnt while they were in training. Vell further honed his fighting skills in desperation to survive while on the run from the Scourge. Once the war ended, they settled into the town and their lives settled as well. Vell's improvements plateaued despite his training and sparring for the past ten years. And of course, the personal developments that were neglected on the run had caught up with him causing him to stay in his safe little circle, forgoing school and friends.

In the back of Keiara's mind, she was alright with Vell taking his time to develop. His childhood had been taken away from him. So a delayed start at a normal life was okay. But it was difficult for people to understand. Most of the ones who would have understood Vell's situation had not made it out alive in the first place. They had not been able to do what Keiara and Vell had done to survive. So what if he acted a bit childish at times?

But Vell was starting to learn how to interact with people properly. Some of the people were not afraid to tell him when he had done something weird. Some even went out of their way to gently show him the proper response. Even sparring with people had developed him somehow. Even though he did not smile or laugh openly, Keiara knew her son was happy.

"D-Damn it!" one of the soldiers said as he crossed the finish line. He promptly dropped to the ground as he used up the little bit of energy left in him to gasp for air. A few others rolled in behind him and found their own spot on the ground.

"All that and you still didn't beat Vell," one of the soldiers gasped on the ground. Her face was planted into the grass, so her insult was muffled.

"I wasn't trying to beat Vell," the runner-up replied after half a minute, catching enough air to speak. "I was trying not to fall too far behind."

The small group of overachievers continued to gasp for air as they slowly recovered. Meanwhile the main group rolled into view. They had not pushed as hard, but they were not much less winded.

"Alright, good job, troopers," Keiara said as they crossed the finish line. Most were pretty winded, but not winded enough to fall flat on their faces like the first group. Keiara let them rest a little before moving on. Out in the open, in full gear, the heat from the day can really get one into trouble. Yes, they need to get used to it, but they also need to take care not to overdo it. So a little rest before the next round of activity was the norm.

But their usual routine was interrupted.

"Instructor Keiara," one of the soldiers said, looking off into the distance. "Looks like two soldiers on horseback."

Keiara looked in the same direction as the soldier. Although she had good sight, this soldier had a better knack for identifying things. "Friendly?" she asked.

After a moment, he responded, "Yup, one of ours."

Even in a safe area like this, where one did not expect an attack, it was still good to be on their toes. This was a subtle part of the training – habits that a soldier should have.

The platoon and the accompanying mercenary instructors waited for the riders to come to them. When they did, one of the soldiers dismounted and the other stayed seated.

"Messenger, sir," the rider who had stayed seated said. "Your presence is required for an important emergency meeting."

This does not bode well, Keiara thought. But there can't be an emergency at the gate because any activity could be seen from where they were. "Do you know what type of emergency it is?"

The rider looked at his fellow rider who had dismounted. Then he sighed. "Not the *real* type of emergency, sir," he said in a low tone. The way he said what he said, and what was left unsaid, told Keiara what she needed. It was really just someone who felt important needing to do something important so that they continued to feel important.

"Understood," she said. She then turned to her training platoon. "You guys know the drill." Her platoon answered in the affirmative. Then she turned her attention to the dismounted rider who offered her the reigns to his horse. "Thank you," she said as she accepted the reigns and mounted the horse.

"You don't need to ride to another group?" Keiara asked the messenger.

"No, sir," he answered. "Your group is the furthest out and the last we needed to bring in. Letting you ride the horse back will help speed things along."

Keiara nodded and they headed back to camp on horseback.

Okay, this is new, Keiara thought as she walked through the double-doors. She entered a large room dominated by a large table. The table had big map of the region – both on the populated side of the Wall and the unpopulated side – with various tokens and documents scattered about.

This was her first time in the actual fort strategy room. It was large enough to comfortably fit a lot of personnel in full-gear. And, right now, even with the amount of people in it, it still was not at full capacity.

This room must have been created for a last-stand in case the fort was overrun.

The sub-commander noticed that Keiara and the messenger had walked in and informed the Commander.

"Looks like we're all here, so let's begin," the Commander announced.

It took a while for the crowd to settle down but it eventually did. The Commander waited patiently and launched into his speech immediately after the noise had died down enough.

It was not good news.

"...So, ladies and gentlemen," the Commander drone on, "since the main force led by Crown Princess, Princess Ainsley II has been delayed indefinitely and with not even an estimated date of arrival..."

Keiara could feel the restlessness in the room that seemed to collectively shout, *Get on with it!* Will we get paid and be sent home? Or will we have an extension?

"...we will use the trained forces here, along with help from our mercenary friends, to start the next stage of our operation..."

"I have a bad feeling about this," someone whispered to one of the mercenaries standing near Keiara. She held the same sentiment.

"...which is to enter the Wall and get a foothold into the territory beyond."

As the Commander said the last line, he made a dramatic gesture and held it. He may have been waiting for an equally dramatic response – clapping, cheering, or something – but instead he got silence.

Keiara could not believe what she just heard. This seat-warmer wanted to take the freshly trained troops, without the main unit, into the territory of one of the deadliest foes known? And he's hoping the mercenaries would be enough to offset the inexperience and the main unit of over 5000 soldiers? Shaking her head in disbelief, Keiara looked around to see if anyone else had broken the spell.

But the silence remained.

This had to be a bad joke, right?

"Hey!" someone yelled from the back of the room. "This isn't what we signed up for. We were brought on as trainers, not front-liners."

That first statement caused the entire room to light up in protests. The cacophony of noise escalated as each loud-mouthed mercenary tried to get their complaints heard over the others. It came to a point where the whole room reverberated because of the volume.

After a long run of this, the volume eventually dropped enough for someone to be heard. Unfortunately it was the suspicious, brownnosing Sub-Commander that had the misfortune to be caught saying something stupid during this lull.

"...but it is combat! Isn't that what you mercenaries live for? Combat and money? Or are you scared of a little fighting?"

The comparatively-tame complaints quickly turned into a rowdy mess of expletives and insults. Someone even threw something at the Sub-Commander.

Keiara was not happy either, but this conference was not going anywhere but down. Someone needed to step in and help wrangle this mess before it sinks the entire ship.

And, as in most cases, she had to be the one to do it.

"Alright!" she yelled, her usual melodious voice changed to a harsher commanding voice. "That's enough. Now settle down."

Most of the mercenaries from her town and those that knew her almost immediately complied with her commands. The ones that did not comply just did not hear her. But the mercenaries who saw her as a frail woman toed the line and squeezed some insults in. They received a rude lesson on who really had heft in this group – and it was not them.

"Shut yer traps!" Tilian roared in a primal voice. Once he made sure that the lesson had been doled out and received he softened his voice and egged Keiara on.

"Thank you, Tilian," she said in her normal voice. With the silence in the room, Keiara did not have to speak much louder than her normal voice to be heard. "Despite how it was delivered, the sentiments were on point: we were contracted to train, not to fight. And with such a drastic change, we can choose to go or not as it is considered an amendment."

The Commander, who had been suspiciously silent throughout the racket, still held the performer's smile that he had when he was giving his earlier speech. As Keiara finished her explanation, he stood for a moment before he began pacing along the front of the room like some great historical figure.

"If you were to look at your contract in detail, you would notice that there are terms for extensions and extra work that may require your expertise," he said. The tone of his voice almost made it sound condescending.

But Keiara had to agree with the Commander on the existence of the extension clause. However, it sounded like he had a different interpretation of it.

"Yes, and those extensions are optional from the base contract," Keiara said with confidence. "And we have completed the base contract which specify the training of the soldiers that are already here, not the ones in the main unit."

Hopefully her statement had covered enough of the possible loopholes that the Commander was planning on using. At the very least, it would show him that she had not glanced over the contract like a typical mercenary might have. It was just one of the reasons that she held such high respect from the guild and other mercenaries who had worked with her.

The Commander had not lost his composure. He took in the statement and meditated on it. Without missing a beat, he continued.

"But the contract requires proof of proper training," he said."

"And that is usually done with simulations and controlled tests," Keiara shot off.

"But what is a better test than actual combat?"

"Actual combat can be too chaotic for training proof. That's why the government and the guilds agree on the simulations and tests," Keiara said. "It's a standard where a contract has to explicitly mention the alternative, and even then it has to go through specific approvals from the government."

The Commander's smile looked more and more forced as Keiara shot down his political finagling. If he had any interest in this training expedition, he would've known that Keiara was not your typical mercenary. Her training and upbringing had made sure of that. Keiara noticed that the fort commander had his eyes closed tightly. To the casual observer, it may have looked like he was bored or frustrated with the argument. To Keiara though, she could see it was an attempt to hold in his laughter at the absurdity of the Commander's words. It was possible that the fort commander had heard the argument earlier as part of the Commander's consul. And when he countered it, he was unceremoniously waved off for 'bad advice'.

Except, from the looks of things, his 'bad advice' was what was happening right now.

"What about your bonus?" the Commander asked.

"What about it?" Keiara shot back.

The Commander just raised an eyebrow and goaded her forward. It looked look like he did not want to give away any more arguments by speaking too much.

It did not matter to Keiara. She knew what she was talking about. "The bonus is for the base contract. Any and *all* extensions that come from this contract is not included as a condition for the bonus," she said.

The Commander's smile had faded by then. His eyes locked onto Keiara, but she was not fazed. The Commander then turned to look at the Sub-Commander. He was clearly furious but also intimidated by Keiara. The Commander sighed, then closed his eyes and twisted his neck in a way that made it pop.

"Fine. I just wanted to give you guys a chance for glorious combat," he said. "To be the first ones in and claim the glory of entering a land that had been given up to the enemy. A chance to retake what had been stolen." He sighed dramatically. "But I did not even imagine that such fine warriors as yourselves would be so... what's the word?... apprehensive to take on the fight." He paused thoughtfully, then continued, "No, that's not the right word. It might be too complicated for you.

What are some alternatives? Lacking courage, fearful, scared..."

"...Chicken?" the Sub-Commander offered innocently.

"Yeeeesss," the Commander said, dragging the word. "Chicken. I did not think such fine warriors would actually be such chickens."

It was an obvious attempt to goad the mercenaries. Some took the bait and offered up meaningless insults, but thankfully most took their cues from a silent, steely-eyed Keiara.

"Well, a chance for glorious combat," the Commander droned on, "for medals, for money, fame, etc. And you guys are too scared to go in. Sorry, too chicken. I guess we'll have to give up on that." He shrugged dramatic again, hands held up and shoulders up as if he offered an imaginary bowl in each hand.

"But think of it this way," he continued with a sinister look. "Once this is open territory, there will be a lot more work required. Most of it will be mercenary work. And if you refuse to take this job, as you're sooo entitled to, then us simple-minded administrators might remember that you were not interested in the work and won't bother to let you know about it. Of course, even if you were to try and get a job, why should we choose you since you've already let us down before? Why won't we take a chance on someone else?"

That's how he was going to play it, Keiara thought. This almost caused her emotions to boil to overflowing. She hated when slime-nosed politicians tried to finagle people into doing their bidding. Worst were those low-level pretend politicians that could not manipulate people into doing their work and instead threatened them. True, both of it was manipulation, but threats were so base and unintelligent that it was nothing more advance than a thug's tactics.

The echoes of the protests included someone saying that the Commander could not do that.

"… Oh, I can," he said with a grin of a make-believe dictator. He then proceeded to spout torrents of unnecessary information about his family accolades and connections, as well as political weight.

Although together the mercenaries were strong in their opinion to not enter the Wall, the threat of their livelihood – where most of the steady jobs came from government contracts – had planted the seeds of doubt in their minds.

"But if you fine soldiers decide to come along, your wages and bonuses would be well more than worth it," the Commander said, his smile returning.

"No use if we're dead…" someone mumbled. But in the silence, the comment seemed to echo like an uncomfortable noise that no one wanted to admit to hearing.

"Oh, no worries, your family will get the full benefits plus a death or permanent injury lump-sum payment," the Sub-Commander added.

It did not help.

The Commander sensed the air and said, "Well, not that we'd want you to die. In any case, we're just clearing the outpost on the other side of the Wall so that the main army will have a foothold when they arrive." He quickly added, "But it is all up to you. You can leave and end your contract, or you can continue the prosperous relationship you have with the government."

And, without accepting another argument, he walked off with a curt farewell and dismissal of the meeting. The startled Sub-Commander quickly regained his senses and followed the Commander so closely that it looked like he was already in the process of brownnosing the Commander.

The atmosphere was so thick, and the stunned silence so dense, that it could be cut with a training sword.

All eyes slowly drifted to Keiara. It took more than a moment for her to realize it while she focused on her thoughts. But when she did, she looked around the room for an answer. Her eyes zeroed in on Captain Wilhelm. And all the eyes were suddenly on him.

Keiara could sense the discomfort in Captain Wilhelm. Any real soldier worth their salt would feel discomfort from being thrown to the wolves like that. To his credit, Captain Wilhelm recovered, albeit with a sigh and a frown.

"Alright ladies and gentlemen," the Captain said, "now you know the plan, make your choices."

He paused and looked around the room, meeting each mercenary with his eyes. "We will discuss high-level strategy. Once that is done, you can go off to decide what you want to do. If you decide to end your contract, proceed to the logistics department located here in the fort to tie things up." The captain nodded at his colleague, the fort commander, and said, "I'm sure you'll be able to take care of them well."

The fort commander nodded in reply. "Sure can," he said. It seemed like he understood what the captain meant. Keiara was glad that there was some competence along the chain of command.

"Once you've decided to stay, we'll go over the strategy in more detail," he said. "Of course, none of you government troops have a choice."

That last line earned him a scattered round of stale laughter. He smiled grimly at his fellow men-at-arms.

"Alright, let's begin."

8

"It's a beautiful day for a slaughter."

"Sorry, Captain Wilhelm, did you say something?" the fort commander asked.

Wilhelm shook his head, both in response and to remove the haze surrounding his thoughts. "Sorry, I shouldn't have said that out loud," he said.

"Said what?" the fort commander responded with a smile.

Captain Wilhelm scoffed.

The two sat on their horses at the staging area in-between the fort and the Wall where they observed the activity around the gate passageway. Soldiers milled about the area in full gear, their nervousness worn on their gauntlets. The mercenaries were solemn, hiding their own nervousness behind rituals and stone faces. Workers still scrambled around, shouting and toiling away, as they completed preparations and defenses on this side of the Wall.

The Wall was thick. What is referred to as the gate is actually a large tunnel in the Wall that is capped by two large gates. In the tunnel, there were sub-gates that became a barrier to the enemy in an effort to slow them down. People operated under the impression that the Scourge would break through – it was just a matter of when.

But then the Wall held.

It was no ordinary wall. The Wall stretched from one end to the other, connecting natural formations and built sections, such as the one at Fort Holden, all the way to the north. A huge chunk of the country had been carved out by the Scourge, but there was a sliver of the northern territories that survived behind the Wall. That sliver slowly opened up as it moved further south, where it eventually curved and headed in a westerly direction. It was almost as if someone had taken a big bite out of the country, leaving an axe-head-shaped curve of territory left to the people. The state of the borders to the other countries and territories past the Wall were unknown. Wilhelm just imagined that the Scourge could not break through, so they moved west into the neighboring territories. The borders to the east and south were usual cordial, helpful even, but no one knew how long that would last.

Thankfully, the Scourge never found its way through bodies of water, at least for now. It was almost impossible to build the Wall on land, especially with the threat of attack. There had been sections that had been partially built, only for the Scourge to have rushed past them. Having to extend the Wall through the northern shores would have been a nightmare.

People had to give up land when the Wall was finally completed because they could not risk losing the resources of building a section only to have the Scourge overrun it before completion. Many High Magisters, already rare, lost their lives building the Wall. However, without their magic, the Wall would be nothing but a carefully-pieced-together pile of materials, a mere stumbling block for the Scourge.

Wilhelm never understood the magic in the Wall, nor did he need to. It just worked. But that did not mean he put his unwavering faith in it. He was thankful for the time it bought, but prepared for the worst.

And now some idiot decided it was time to tempt fate and open the Wall.

"How many lives were lost building and protecting this thing?" he said. "How many lives did we have to leave behind because we needed to seal the Walls? Even if they knew the sacrifice was for the greater good, how many men, women, children even, were lost to seal the Wall? And now, we open it to take a peek and make sure it's clear for the fat cats to be first to indulge their greed."

The fort commander chuckled. "I guess I'm rubbing off on you," he said. "So much for just being a soldier."

"No offense, but I don't want any of you rubbing on me," Wilhelm responded with a grin, "or rubbing off on me."

The fort commander chuckled again.

Wilhelm's eyes met Instructor Keiara's and he nodded in her direction as he wiped the grin off his face. He suddenly felt guilty for being in slightly higher spirits than she was. Especially when her eyes betrayed her and showed a hint of fear.

Not fear of the enemy, like a lot of the soldiers and mercenaries had in their eyes – hidden or not – it was different fear; the fear for her son, Vell.

Instructor Keiara... she was an interesting one. In the stereotypical world of the soldier of fortune, she wouldn't have made the picture. Lean, elegant, and a stern gentleness of a matriarch; no one would picture someone of her nature roughing it out with the tumblers and rousers that made up the imagined picture of mercenaries. Yet somehow, not only was she one of them, she had the most weight among them. It was a living contrast: apart from them, yet a part of them.

Then there was Vell, her protégé. If skill determined rank, Wilhelm would be reporting to Vell. But so would the Commander and Sub-Commander.

But with this whole mess, most people would have stood down and would not have wanted to be first. Instructor Keiara instead faced her fear and volunteered to be on the front line – the very front. Wilhelm had been reluctant to put her in front because of her sway with the bulk of the mercenaries. In fact, he was surprised that she even stayed to extend the contract. But it made sense to Wilhelm to have the most experienced out front so that it increases the overall plan's chance for success. And of course, the Commander agreed wholeheartedly. Why waste the precious troops they trained and equipped when they could just use the mercenaries who were used to dangerous jobs? The Commander even commended Wilhelm for thinking of such a brilliant strategy.

Wilhelm sighed.

Instructor Keiara was put in charge of the front lines.

"Don't worry, I'll have proper scouts up front so I won't be right in front," she had said.

And then she asked him, Captain Wilhelm, to take care of her son if anything were to happen to her. The sudden weight of that statement had almost pushed Wilhelm to the ground.

"I can't do that," he had said.

After a bit of back and forth (not in his favor), Instructor Keiara relented and said to take care of him here and see him home safely. It was still a tall order, but not as tall as taking care of him the rest of his life.

It was not easy to commit to. Unlike a lot of others, when Wilhelm commits, he commits. But that may be why Instructor Keiara felt she could ask that of him.

At least I'll be free of life-long obligations if I no longer had life, he thought.

And then he sighed again.

It was not the type of thoughts Wilhelm should have had at this point. His thoughts should have been on success.

"Looks like they're ready, Captain," the fort commander said. Apparently the word had come in while Wilhelm was distracted by his thoughts.

He sighed.

Thoughts of success, he thought – even if success meant just living yet another day.

"Alright, ladies and gentlemen," he hollered. "Let's get this show on the road."

The whole show took a bit of time to get on the road. With the amount units and other moving parts involved, it was to be expected. And that was assuming they were not reluctant to get underway in the first place. But no one really wanted to open the gate, or more accurately, no one wanted to be the first to be killed by the Scourge after over ten years of silence.

The scouts entered the tunnel first and helped open the inner gates along the way. The maintenance personnel from the fort, accompanied by additional units from the government forces, checked the integrity and readiness of the tunnel and its supporting offshoots. This was done with regular intervals over the years as part of maintaining the readiness level, so this was close to routine for the fort.

Once that was completed, the maintenance units continued on to the set of gates on the far side of the tunnel, close to the Scourge side of the Wall. This part of the process was not routine to them. They would have normally been accompanied by High Magisters, but none were dispatched to help them this time.

Tensions were high, but the unknown made it even higher. The normal precautions were in place and greatly enhanced to offset the unknown. Thankfully, things went well, and after a bit of maintenance work, the tunnel was given the all-clear sign.

Although the tunnel was big and spacious, the soldiers and mercenaries packed the tunnel to near-claustrophobic levels. It did not seem like a good idea to Wilhelm, but he understood the need for it. If the Scourge attacked, and the defenders in the front flee, it would just cause chaos that would kill more people than the Scourge would. Packing them tight would also allow the back to take some of the load when defending, and it would also prevent the Scourge from leaking through and causing havoc in the middle of the formation. Basically, this formation was a battering ram made of people; if the front or the middle crumbles, then the whole thing falls apart.

The risk, of course, was when an intentional retreat was called, either people in front were sacrificed to let the others escape, or the retreat would be too slow to be effective.

But Wilhelm had to put his mind on success. He could prepare for failure, but not be crippled by its hypotheticals. A soldier should do rather than not do. But higher up the chain, there is more weight to that decision. Not only how it affects the world, but how it affects the troops under one's command. And Wilhelm, although he had risen up the chain, wanted – needed – to remember his roots. He would normally be upfront with the rest of the troops, even if there were mercenary elements. Unfortunately, this time he could not join them in front. He had to sit back and watch from the relative safety of the fort's shadow.

Well intentioned, Wilhelm thought as he remembered the Commander's explicit orders that kept him at the back. The Commander had wanted to make sure the Captain was protected in case things did not go very well. It was... touching, in a weird sort of way. The Commander was a figurehead and was not expected to actually make any major command decisions. He may be incompetent, or merely inexperienced and untrained. Maybe if he were to get experience and have good people to help him make decisions, he might be a competent leader. In his own way, he cared for those under his command, but it was tainted by the privilege and entitlement of aristocracy.

Still, to the troops, the fact of the matter was that the Commander did not make the best decisions. And that simply meant that the troops could not trust him completely because his decisions were not always right, even as grey as most outcomes are expected to be. Doubt in combat, even if a little, could mean the difference between success and failure... or life and death.

Then, the moment arrived.

"Breaching!" the call echoed, carried by different voices so all could hear.

Wilhelm's heart went silent, cold. The only sound he could hear was the ringing of silence in his ears. The vibration of the air, as he liked to imagine it. It gave him comfort that the silence was not emptiness.

He could feel the cold from his still heart spreading out from his chest. His muscles tensed, both locked in position yet poised to spring in any direction. All he could do was stare into the dimly-lit tunnel, all the way to the end, and wish that this was over.

Then a sound echoed from the other side of the tunnel, like a large hammer had dropped. What accompanied it was a long, agonizing chorus of wails and groans originating from vocals of long ago. The sound was terrifying, and Wilhelm had to constantly remind his instinctive self that it was just the sound of an old door opening on old hinges. But his instincts continued fighting against Wilhelm, calling him a liar. Wilhelm could only imagine how much more challenging it was for those actually inside the tunnel to hold on to their wits.

Finally, Wilhelm could see the light at the end of the tunnel.

The Wall was open.

And what greeted them was silence.

Everything froze for what seemed like forever and a day. The silence was amplified by expectation.

Damn it! I wish I was up front, Wilhelm screamed to himself.

According to the strategy meetings, the first up were scouts – mercenary scouts; ones with plenty of experience – to carefully creep forward so that they could scan the area for the Scourge and pull back the operation if needed.

But it was agonizing for Wilhelm to sit in the back and wait for news. Time seemed to remind Wilhelm of each passing moment with pain.

Even though the scouts crept forward, the main column did not move. The extra distance in-between the scouts and the heavy units in the front of the column were to allow the column to brace for an attack before the enemy attacked them, using the scouts as both a signal and bait. But the column had not moved.

Patience was the name of the game here. The gate had not been opened in over ten years. As far as anyone on the other side was concerned, this was just another day.

"What's the hold up, Captain?" a loud voice galloped in on a horse. "Why have we not moved forward?"

Of course, the Commander appears with his lackey in tow at the most tedious stage of the operation.

"As per the strategy meetings, the mercenary scouts are making sure the area is safe to proceed," Wilhelm said. He tried to close any loops that the Commander might use to ask another unnecessary question.

But the Commander still asked another question; this one was more stupid than the Captain gave him credit for. "Well, why is it taking so long?"

"Sir, it takes time for scouts to check everything," Wilhelm said, holding back his frustration as well as he could. "They have to check everything, and make sure what they haven't checked yet is not something that will kill them or alert the enemy to their presence."

The Commander was in a mood, apparently.

"I was observing the whole thing from the fort," the Commander said. "I had enough time to be bored, then eat a leisurely meal, and come back."

We're not your damn entertainment, Wilhelm thought.

"I even got the horses ready and rode down here, and you still haven't moved forward!" the Commander continued.

It took Wilhelm almost all his leftover energy and mental fortitude to prevent himself from sighing.

"It's just the way these operations go, sir," the fort commander jumped in. Wilhelm silently appreciated the effort his colleague made to shoulder the burden. "The reports and the stories don't usually mention how long some of these operational stages are."

He was right, but that did not mean that the Commander and the Sub-Commander took it any less offensively.

The Commander's face grimaced for a long moment. It looked like he was trying to hold in an outburst. A tactic he learnt from whatever elitist institution he was educated in. Unfortunately, he was bad at it.

"What are you saying, Fort Commander Mason?" he said calmly but on edge. "Are you implying that you have more experience than I do and that I have only read about these things in books and have no real knowledge of them? Or maybe you are trying to say that you have more combat experience than me and therefore I am not worthy of asking you questions. And maybe it's true that I don't have experience, but how the hell am I supposed to get experience if I can't participate in combat?" The volume and ferocity of the Commander as he spat out his thoughts increased steadily until his final sentence was spat out in rage.

"T-That's…" the fort commander stuttered.

Wilhelm felt terrible that his friend had stepped in front of him and received the brunt of the blow on his behalf.

"Sir, with respect, that's not what the fort commander was trying to say," Wilhelm said. "He was just stating that these things take time and patience is needed. If there was anything wrong, you'd be told."

"W-With respect!?" the Sub-Commander stepped in and blurted. "As if your attitude has any respect in it, but maybe that's why you had to explicitly say it."

Wilhelm did not mean it that way. He really meant it respectfully, though admittedly he did not always respect these two seat warmers. Wilhelm just treated it as a glancing blow, something he might have deserved at another time but not now.

However, the wry man did not stop flapping his gums.

"A-And you think you're so experience? Actually seen combat against the Scourge?" the Sub-Commander continued, his stutter rose to the surface as his anger did. "Yeah, you did see combat against the Scourge… from a tower far away as you watched the Scourge ravage your fellow soldiers protecting the lines, and as you watched villages and even villagers sacrificed so that you and your friends could retreat."

The statements hit Wilhelm like a blow to the back of the head. Then it hit him again when his memories flooded in – memories of exactly what the Sub-Commander had described. Wilhelm was forced to stay put under orders and ensure a secure evacuation route, for both civilians and military. But he always felt the guilt of having to watch from afar. And then, the guilt of surviving.

But his friends did not retreat. No... in fact, that jumped into the fray when the lines fell back and time needed to be bought. They forced Wilhelm to retreat with the remaining soldiers. "The wounded needed someone to help them," they had said. And then they jump, some even literally jumped off the wall and towers, into the Scourge.

Wilhelm's combat experience against the Scourge amounted to just a kill or two. Even then, he could not take full credit. He got a few hits in, but it was a group effort by desperate men and women running towards sanctuary behind the Wall.

In a haze, as his memories flooded his vision and occupied his mind, Wilhelm had somehow grabbed the Sub-Commander's collar with his hands and yanked him off his horse. It was a good thing the Sub-Commander was tall, or his neck would've been the only thing holding him up in Wilhelm's hands. Sometime between when the Sub-Commander had so brazenly berated Wilhelm to when Wilhelm woke from his daze, the Sub-Commander's face had gone from angry-defiance to terrified.

"That's enough," the Commander yelled. "Sub-Commander, that is crossing the line." Wilhelm let go of the Sub-Commander as he realized what he was doing. The commander then turned to Wilhelm and said, "And you, Captain, although the insult to you and especially your fellow soldiers were uncalled for, please keep your manners about you."

As if you are one to speak, Wilhelm scoffed in his mind. He wasn't going to push it though, because the Commander was right about keeping decorum in place when treating with officers of a higher rank.

"We'll leave the operation to you," the Commander said, "I just wanted to know what was going on. But I trust that you are following the strategies we've already gone over at length."

And then they rode off.

Wilhelm waited a long moment before he let out a sigh. He closed his eyes and titled his head up as he twisted it from one side to the other in an attempt to relieve the tension built up in his neck. After along moment, he finally lowered his head and looked around. His eyes met the fort commander's as he stared at Wilhelm with a look of mild incredulousness. Then Wilhelm looked around and saw that a lot of the people around him were looking at him with the same type of look.

"What?" he asked, loud enough for most people around him to hear.

The replies he received were a mix bag of 'nothings' and apologies.

Wilhelm turned to the fort commander. "Seriously, what?"

The fort commander laughed. "I can't believe the Commander was even able to string together a coherent response, let alone a rebuke, after what you said."

"You mean, with pulling the Sub-Commander off his horse?" Wilhelm said. "I barely even knew I did that."

The fort commander looked at Wilhelm in disbelief. "You really don't remember?"

"The pulling him off? Not really, just that I had somehow grabbed him."

"You don't remember what you did after grabbing him?"

Wilhelm shook his head.

"You roared in his face," the fort commander said, still laughing. "Something about insulting you instead of your friends or whatever, and how they died protecting useless intellectuals like him." He laughed again. "I'm pretty sure everyone, even those in the tunnel, heard you. Probably all of them have fantasized about yelling at them like you did. Maybe not as much roaring though." His laughter did not seem like it was going to let up.

Wilhelm was honestly embarrassed at his outburst, even more so because he did not remember it. The rage must have been churning inside of him to come out like that.

A soldier from the tunnel came to them and gave them a report.

The area around the gate on the other side was clear. Even the base was clear. No sign of the Scourge at all.

None at all.

9

It was unbelievable – amazing, even. Somehow, the Wall had held.

Before breaching the gate, tensions were high. Keiara knew she did not want to be there, but she also knew she had to. If the mission had a chance of success, she was going to be there to help increase that chance.

But when they finally breached the gate, and she followed the scouts out of it, they were greeted by silence. Not the eerie type of silence, but a gentle, peaceful one. That fact made the situation eerie.

So the scouts looked and looked. They carefully crept forward and scanned every new piece of sector in their visual range. Then they checked it twice, and then they confirmed it with their fellow scouts as they crept forward. It was agonizingly slow, but the stillness had made the scouts extra cautious.

However, all they found were wooden structures in various states of decay and neglect; fallen bits of armor and equipment, some may have even held a body at one time, but instead held skeletal remains; and a fairly decent, though overgrown, perimeter with defensive structures in place.

When they cleared the outpost, some of the scouts were brave enough to even extend their search past the wooden walls of the perimeter.

Whoever had planned the base defenses must've had experience defending against the Scourge. It was hard to tell if the base was built in a hurry, but the thick walls were made from solid timber. It even looked like the outer wall was doubled or tripled up in thickness. In front of the wall was a vast field of emptiness – clean sightlines all around – which eventually led to a heavily forested area. But anyone who tried to cross that field left themselves exposed for a very long time, plenty of time for the defenders in the base to bring them down.

Thankfully, the scouts and their bravado ended just before the field hit the forest. Any further and it would risk straining the lines. It would be very difficult to help them that far out without a solidified base on this side of the Wall. And at that point, the rest of the breaching team had just streamed into the compound. They too had their own checks to do – partially protocol, partially for their own sanity.

Keiara had not realized it at the time, but as the day wore on and night fell, the tension she had felt, even before she left for the mission with Vell, had faded away. There still was the usual nagging awareness an experienced soldier had on the field, but it was no longer the heavy burden that had weighed on her mind and heart for so long.

Still, night was a time when the Scourge was deadliest. Not that they were nocturnal, but rather because it was hard to detect them and see their movements. Usually, you'd want to get as much warning as one could to defend and prepare against an attack. It often took a lot of time for soldiers to band together during the chaos and get their defenses tight. Any kink, any crumble, and the Scourge could bring down their defenses in seconds. The Scourge's quickness and agility made it easy to exploit almost any weakness in the defenses. And of course, the darkness of night made it harder for the defenders to see. It often was the difference between incredibly difficult and impossible.

But so far, everything seemed quiet. The units in the forward base were on extra high alert. Soldiers were not allowed to be alone – the minimum was in pairs, and even that was a risk no one took. The priority was to repair the defensive wall at the perimeter, but the units walked forward slowly to make sure all ground claimed in the forward base was safe. Now that the perimeter wall was back to at least the minimum level of security and darkness had fallen, the support units pulled in to the camp and focused on repairing or rebuilding the key structures in the base.

The soldiers and mercenaries slept in shifts throughout the night, but Keiara doubted that anyone had a good rest that night. It was easier the next few nights as the quiet continued and the defenses were rebuilt and reinforced. Someone even suggested reinforcing the base of the wall with metal and concrete to reinforce the already-reinforced wooden wall. Keiara thought it was a good idea, to go above and beyond. They even put in large wooden stakes at the base of the wall to prevent the Scourge from rushing it. A veteran soldier or mercenary must've suggested the tactic since it was not common knowledge.

But what was a welcomed reprieve for some, was a painful wait for others. Just a few short days after the breach, a strategy meeting was called.

"…And everything is ahead of schedule, leaving us enough time to solidify our defenses even further," one of the leads of the support units said. "In a few more days, we can even start putting up a string of exploratory outposts into the surrounding areas, all well within line of sight of each other. Our troops can use those as staging areas to push forward or fallback points to rally during a defensive pullback."

The meeting was held in one of the bigger buildings on the base. It was a far cry from the opulence of the fort's strategy room, which is saying much because the fort was not exactly opulent either. Since the room was smaller, the meeting did not call everyone in – just the main leaders or representatives. Even the fort commander was absent from the meeting.

The lead who had just given his report looked pleased with himself. And he should have. His team, and the others, they all had done a fantastic job of shoring up the defenses and facilities. They may have put the building they were currently holding the meeting on a lower level on the priority list, but it was all very well done. It helped that things were quiet and they did not have to worry about building things while dealing with the chaos of an enemy attack.

All in all, the expedition beyond the Wall, even without the main unit's support, had gone exceedingly well.

But it did not look like things were well according to the Commander's face.

And the troubled look on the Commander's face troubled Keiara. Knowing his desire for accolades and glory, Keiara worried that the Commander was going to try to push things as far as he could.

An uncomfortable silence settled in the room, even after the lead of the support unit had long sat down and the polite applause had dissipated.

"I take it there is no one else with anything pertinent to report?" Captain Wilhelm said, breaking the uncomfortable silence.

No one responded.

Captain Wilhelm turned to the Commander. "Commander, that about wraps up the reports, sir," he said. The Commander's gaze was off into the unknown, his face scrunched up into strained boredom. He was not paying attention. The

Captain continued. "We're fortunate that the Scourge has not attacked and that we have been able to rebuild and get a firm foothold into this side of the Wall.

"Now all we have to do is wait for the main force to arrive," Captain Wilhelm ended. Keiara silently hoped that this would be it – no stupidity from the Commander.

But that hope soon evaporated away.

The Commander stood up in an exaggerated, languid way and tilted his head at the Captain. "Bravo," he said, stretching out the ending of the word and clapping like a tired seal, his face distorted into a type of tired sarcasm. "Great job everyone," he continued. "Rebuilding structures that were already there, and strengthening walls to hide behind. Bravo."

The support staff shifted uncomfortably in their seats. The soldiers and mercenaries were more composed, but Keiara could still feel the shift in the air. Even the Sub-Commander's eyes darted around nervously. The Commander no longer held and hint of the decorum that his privileged upbringing had afforded him. It had disappeared entirely. His mask had fallen off leaving the true face open to the world.

"But where was the combat? Where was the action?" he said. "What was the point of spending all that time and money to prepare for this expedition, only for it to be a walk in the park to a lovely picnic in the forest?" He sighed. "There is no point to sitting here, safe. We will not get recognition for this. Why are you so satisfied with this… this… lack of events?"

He turned dramatically to his audience, begging them silently for an answer. And he received it – silence.

"Sir, everything went better than expected," Captain Wilhelm said. "We completed our objectives flawlessly with no casualties and ahead of schedule. What more do you want?"

The Commander flung his head in the Captain's direction and glared at him with glowering eyes. "Completed flawlessly?" he growled, almost sounding like a creature from beyond. "The whole point of this exercise was to test your troops in combat! And there was no combat." The Commander pounded the palm of his hand into his chest furiously. "And how do we test if the troops have improved without combat!? That was the whole point of spending gobs of money and time on them to make them better warriors. We're wasting them. Wasting them!"

It took a while for the last sentence, which was screamed, to fade out in the room. It still echoed softly when the Captain risked retribution by speaking up. "Wasn't the objective to safely capture and rebuild the forward base?"

The Commander made an angry gurgling sound in his throat. The volume reached that of a roar, but it was never let loose from his throat. "How many times do I have to say it?" he said menacingly.

"The objective was to test the troops in combat against the Scourge." He coughed and straightened himself. "Securing the base and rebuilding it was just to give the troops something to fight for."

Keiara had seen this before. She called it low-level politics. It was basically a crude method of trying to manipulate people into doing things or not doing things. The very basic method was violence or threats. Taking it beyond that level made people feel like a budding politician instead of a simple thug. But really, both were so basic that Keiara grouped it into the same category.

Still, just because Keiara knew something or had seen it before did not mean that it was common knowledge or even common sense. It was a point that often caused Keiara's heart to ache. Even the amount she knew was so little compared to what her progenitors considered common knowledge. It just showed how much society had fallen and how much time and effort was lost to rediscover what was once taken for granted.

Keiara looked around and gauged the feeling of the room. As expected, the soldiers were not happy with the idea that, as part of some grand strategy, they were expected to go into combat and some were even expected to die. What jabbed them in the gut was that since none of that happened, their commander's master plan had failed and he was upset with them... for surviving.

Captain Wilhelm did not look like he could tolerate the incompetence any longer.

"Sir, you intended for us to go into combat, even die, to test us out and for you to get commendations? And then, when things went smoothly without combat, you pout like a child?"

Keiara winced when she heard his choice of words. Captain Wilhelm had been a stalwart example of how to keep emotions in check, even when dealing with a glory hound like the Commander. And now his stony resolve had cracked.

But as expected, when someone acting like a child was called a child, they did not take it very well.

"A child!?" the Commander roared again. "You, a coward, so intent on being so far from combat, calls me a child?"

"W-With all due..." Wilhelm started.

But the Commander cut him off.

"Oh come off your 'with all due respect' shill," he said with genuine disgust in his face. "I know you don't have any respect for me, and guess what? I don't have respect for you either! Not for some soldier stuck sucking on the teat of the government and the people, but won't enter combat to save lives. That's why no one has heard of you. I've only dealt with you because that's what we're taught to do. Even if the people are of a lower position, lower intelligence, lower means, we are still supposed to treat them graciously. That's the difference between kings and peasants."

The Captain's face was indifferent again, but his eyes look like they burned with fury. The Commander just stared him down, threatening him to speak so he could shoot him down again. When the Captain decided to face the threat and open his mouth, the Commander shot him down before the Captain could even get a word out.

"So what do you have to say for yourself? You sat in the back while the soldiers breached the gate and stormed the forward base. Just like how you sat back and watch your comrades and innocent people get slaughtered by the Scourge."

The Sub-Commander's face twitched.

That... that isn't right, Keiara thought. Not only did he bring out something from the Captain's past, but Keiara was there when the Commander ordered the Captain to the back for safety reasons. That is why Keiara volunteered in the first place, because the Commander had wanted to place the mercenaries upfront, possibly so that they could get killed first.

The Captain remained silent as the Commander stared him down, the tip of their noses just out of reach of each other. When the Commander felt that he had won, he backed off with a victorious smirk.

The Commander turned to face his audience, and spread out his arms in a dramatic fashion. "Worry not, friends and fellow comrades, we will make another chance for us to gain distinctions," he said with a self-indulgent grin. "We will start scouting out the surrounding areas and reclaim the lost territories. We will link up with another gate and make trade great again. Those soldiers in the main unit will look at what we've achieved and we will be rewarded for our excellence!"

The man was so full of himself, and so intent on betting everything for glory. Who did he need to impress? The Princess?

The Commander held a dramatic pose, like a showman expecting applause to shower down on him.

Instead, someone pierced the silence with a single muttered word.

"Bullshit."

The stunned commander slowly exited showman mode in disbelief. "What?"

"I said this is bullshit," a mercenary from the back said.

The Commander's fury needed to find its target. "Who said that!?" he demanded.

A mercenary put his hand up. "I did," he said.

The Commander reoriented himself and said, "Well, you don't have to join in. Get out."

"Gladly," he said as he promptly walked out. But before he exited, he turned and said to the group, "Don't let this fool get you killed. Go home to your families. Glory is bullshit."

"And you'll never work for the government again," the Commander said.

"Fine, make sure to get my name right," he said.

Keiara doubted that the Commander knew the mercenary's name.

Unfortunately, he was the only one that walked out. Keiara knew why she was staying. She needed to make sure that the expedition went well so that she and Vell would not have to run from the Scourge anymore. Even if the idiots in charge screwed up, she was going to see it through.

But no one else had to stay.

Maybe the other mercenaries had seen her resolve, mistook it for what it was, and decided not to leave.

The Commander eyed everyone in the room. When he was finally satisfied, he said, "Looks like everyone else is ready to go. We just need to discuss strategy."

"Commander, I strongly suggest…" the Captain started.

But he was instantly cut off with just as sudden an attitude change by the Commander. "Did I not make myself clear?" he yelled. "No one… NO ONE wants to hear your opinion or strategic advice. We're here to fight, and you'll just have us sitting behind the defenses with you in the very back!"

Keiara had to give the Captain accolades – even thought he was just unfairly humiliated by the Commander, he still had the guts to try to set the strategy. Very admirable.

The Captain just looked at the Commander with a stony-faced expression. The silent exchange lasted an uncomfortable amount of time. Then the Commander spoke. "Get out."

The Captain flinched slightly, but then promptly did a stiff about-face without his usual sigh and swiftly walked out.

The Commander turned to his audience again, but he clearly had trouble regaining his composure.

"S-Sir?" the Sub-Commander interjected. The Commander turned to him with unfocused eyes. "The strategy?" the Sub-Commander said, unsure if he was crossing the line as well.

The Commander looked like he was in deep thought and his eyes remained unfocused.

"Just send them out. They'll eventually run into something," he said. He then walked out of the meeting, leaving everyone dumbfounded. Some even had their jaws literally wide open in astonishment.

"What the hell?" someone yelled. That shook the shock out of the group.

"That's no strategy!"

"Who's going to run strategy? Because that was bullshit."

The protests were loud and clear. Keiara couldn't agree more. The Commander had told his most senior and experience soldier to get the hell out, then the Commander walked out after muttering to himself.

But the Sub-Commander grabbed everyone's attention. Not by yelling or shouting – but by doing the unexpected.

"I'm sorry for that," he said as he bowed deeply to the group. "That was very unbecoming of someone of his station. I apologize on his behalf." He held the bow for a long period before having the courage to come back up. And when he did, his eyes looked… solemn and apologetic, genuinely so.

"L-Let me get some better directions and come back to you. Please wait here for just a few minutes." He then hurried towards the door.

"You want us to wait?"

"Yes, please, just for a little while. I will come back with more information or send back word if I can't resolve this quickly."

A few dissatisfied grunts went up from the crowd, to which the Sub-Commander said a quick 'thank you' before rushing out.

"What kind of garbage have we got ourselves into, lass," Tilian said to Keiara.

"Maybe you should get out and go home to your family."

"Maybe," Tilian mused. "Are you staying?"

"Yes."

"Why?"

"I have my reasons," Keiara said to Tilian with her signature smile.

"Well, I can't let you go alone in this," he said, crossing his arms.

"Don't go dying on my account," Keiara retorted.

"Don't worry, lass, I'm not going down that easy."

Keiara scoffed. Tilian let out a hearty laugh.

True to his word, the Sub-Commander came back within a reasonable amount of time and took charge of the meeting. For once, the Sub-Commander did not look like some nervous, sniveling propinquity of the Commander. Somehow, being in charge had granted the Sub-Commander more confidence, which truthfully brought his confidence level to that of a normal person. Still, it was a stark improvement and it made Keiara wonder how many people were pushed aside because they had slightly lower social standing.

"So it seems that we will need to come up with a strategy to enact the Commander's orders," the Sub-Commander said. "However, I know very well that I'm nowhere near as experienced in matters of combat or deployment strategy as everyone else here. So, with that being said, please do offer your suggestions as we move along."

And that was not just lip-service. Although he had a rough plan in mind, which actually was not too bad on its own, he was willing to thoughtfully listen and discuss suggestions offered by the gathered group. One caveat was that it had to be presented in a civil manner, mostly without insults and emotions.

"As someone who is inexperienced, I need a proper explanation to the logic of your suggestion so I can understand it," he said, "or at least feel like I understand it." And phrases like that helped disarm the group and brought back a semblance of respect and even amiability.

"Look, I understand the Commander wants to show progress. That is what is important to him, so he can show he is capable," the Sub-Commander explained. There were some things that were clearly left out, like personal ambition and even the pressures of the elite to keep their standing, but the majority of the group understood what the Sub-Commander was trying to do. "But I also understand that the Scourge is not an easy opponent. I don't think anyone is in a rush to face them.

"So what we need to do is to move forward, show progress, but we don't have to be overly aggressive." The Sub-Commander looked everyone in the eye to see if anyone had any objections. Instead, he received nods of agreement and even approval. "If we've cleared enough by the time the main unit arrives, we will be held with higher regard. That means that our soldiers will become the more experienced soldiers." This brought a few smiles to the young soldiers in the group. "And for the mercenaries, well, it means you guys did a good job and the perception of you all will improve dramatically.

"Now, let's go over the plan again as well as contingencies," the Sub-Commander said, wrapping up the meeting.

Not bad, Keiara thought to herself.

The plan was good and well thought out. The units that will go into the forest were to be mixed – mercenaries with soldiers. If possible, the mercenaries who had trained the soldiers would be grouped together since they already knew each other. Any problems with the individual arrangements could be discussed and units could be traded or even held back at the outpost. From there, during daylight hours only, the troops would move forward slowly along the most sensible pathways and clear the areas. Once they find an area that is far enough away but not out of line of sight from an outpost tower or the main base, they would mark it for the support units to build a mini-base. Units will either guard the support units as they build or they will rotate out with another group as they continue to move forward.

So, basically stepping forward slowly and extending the base with mini-outposts as fallback points.

Not bad at all, Keiara thought.

"Good?" the Sub-Commander asked the group. He received a warm, affirmative response. "Then get prepped and rested. We'll head out tomorrow morning."

10

It was a long while before Wilhelm felt better. Even the next day, the day of the operation, he still felt terrible. And his fresh wounds had reopened when he was told, in no uncertain terms, to sit this operation out.

Without the responsibility of the whole base and the whole mission on his shoulders, he felt aimless and found himself wandering from place to place. It was a good chance for him to see the troops and support personnel on a personal level and chat with them. He was able to see how things carried on like clockwork even without him. But eventually he found himself in a place of comfort, sparring with the troops.

He had always wanted to do exceedingly well at tasks he was given. Swordsmanship and combat was no exception. And he worked hard, trained hard, to be as good as he was. But he wasn't selfish. He taught what he knew and coached people on how to better do what they already knew. Some people appreciated it, and some hated it for a multitude of reasons. The sons and daughters of the upper-class saw it as a chance for some peasant to humiliate them, and those that thought they were good saw it as something to disregard. Someone of his age that just sat at the humble rank of Captain and still serving in the government forces must have had something wrong with him.

And Wilhelm had started to question if that was really the case. However, his mind could not settle enough to find an answer.

But the simplicity of sparring calmed him enough to keep his mind off of his mental crisis. Eventually, he found a great partner that challenged him enough mentally, but also had the stamina to keep up with an extended sparring session – not to mention someone who had the time to do so. It also helped that his sparring partner did not speak much either.

Maybe Vell needed to take his mind off of things as well, Wilhelm thought as he continued in the rhythm of attack and defense. He knew Vell wasn't trying hard, but occasionally he'll throw in a maneuver or attack that would keep Wilhelm on his toes, and Wilhelm occasionally did the same.

But since the expedition teams had already gone out earlier that morning, everyone on the base had basically gone on standby waiting for the reports to come in. Wilhelm's official duty was to head the defenses at the base, but really he was sidelined. A part of him hated it, but a small part – one that Wilhelm refused to admit – was happy that he did not have to go out and, possibly, face the Scourge. That small part kept the fresh tongue lashing from the Commander, and Wilhelm's own doubts and shame, from shaking off of his heart.

"Vell, what do you think of me?" he said as they continued to spar.

"I think you're distracted," he said.

The unexpectedly present answer caught Wilhelm off-guard and caused him to laugh.

"Don't worry, so am I," Vell continued.

Wilhelm chuckled.

"Well, what's on your mind, son?" Wilhelm asked.

It did not look like Vell had heard the question, or was even thinking of it, but eventually he did muster a half answer.

"It's hard to describe," he said. "I'm worried about my mother, and her friends, as well as the troops out there with them." He paused. "But I'm also going through the tactical reasons why we're pushing so far forward, or why my mother wanted to do so in the first place."

"Maybe she wants to keep you safe," Wilhelm offered with a downward slash of his sword. "Or the money is good."

"The money is good," Vell mused, eyes unfocused, but very readily defending the slash. "But we don't really need the money."

"Are you worried about the Scourge?" Wilhelm asked.

Another pause. "I think so."

That took Wilhelm back a bit. "You think so?" he said. "What do you mean?"

"Well," Vell started, his motions stopping for a moment, "everyone says the Scourge is scary and how they are terrified of them, but I don't know if I feel that way. I know I should be scared... maybe I am... but I don't know if that is because everyone tells me I should be scared, or if I am really scared of them."

That sounded strange to Wilhelm. Of course everyone is scared, right? Was he scared before he saw the Scourge firsthand? Or did the fear come after he had seen them? Surprisingly, Vell's answer set off a chain of uncertainty in his mind. When he realized this, he laughed.

"Now I'm not sure if I'm scared of the Scourge or not," he said with a laugh.

What should have been a tension-filled morning turned into a leisurely one, at least for Captain Wilhelm and Vell. After a bit more sparring, they decided to take a break from the base's defensive line and have lunch. The lunch turned into a long one as soldiers and personnel in the different rotation groups swapped in and out of conversation with the Captain. In the back of his mind, Wilhelm felt guilty for taking time off, even though he was basically ordered to. But it was a nice change of pace to spend time with the men and women on a personal level without the weight and the hustle of command.

Taking advantage of the time he had been given, Wilhelm let himself enjoy the flow of the base – both being a part from it but also a part of it, like a still object amongst a rushing stream or an element outside of the flow of time. If someone gave him the time of day out of their busy schedule, he obliged. Eventually he felt rested enough and restless enough to get himself geared up again and head out to spar with his silent companion, Vell.

"You sure you're okay sparring with an old man like me again?" Wilhelm asked Vell.

"Sure," Vell replied. "It's better than training by myself all day."

"All day? What do you mean?"

"Normally at home I would do chores then train for several hours before eating dinner and then going to bed," Vell explained as he adjusted one of his shoulder pieces.

"So, sparring and training for hours, all day, is normal to you?" Wilhelm asked.

"Yes, Captain."

Wilhelm shook his head with an incredulous smile.

"Maybe if I had known that, I would've started sparring with you sooner," he replied.

But Vell had suddenly stopped walking. He looked... distracted, and even a little confused. His eyebrows were furrowed and his eyes flickered back and forth as if searching for something on the ground, but it was clear to Wilhelm that Vell was not searching the ground but rather his mind.

"What's wrong?" Wilhelm asked.

Before Vell could respond, one of the defenders of the base perimeters interrupted the Captain.

"Captain Wilhelm," the defender said as he recovered from his trot, "there's something going on at the tree line... animals or something."

"Animals?" Wilhelm asked, his own brows furrowed now. Since they had been past the Wall, they had not seen any animals, birds or critters, which added to the eerie atmosphere when the troops first arrived.

Just then, Vell rushed past both Wilhelm and the defender, towards the front gate of the base. Without thinking, Wilhelm followed him.

It worried Wilhelm that Vell's face, normally stoic – expressionless – had contorted into an expression akin to worry and disbelief.

"What is it, Vell," Wilhelm asked as they both clamored up the stairs to the top of the base walls. Vell did not answer.

When they reached the top, Vell looked out, past the empty grounds and into the distant tree lines, and seemed to be searching for something.

The defender that had reported to Wilhelm came up, huffing and puffing, to the battlement where Wilhelm and Vell stood. "Sir, the tree line over there. Do you see them?" Wilhelm could not see what he was talking about.

Wilhelm strained to look. His gut suddenly felt a tinge of nervousness, and it actually annoyed Wilhelm that his abdomen was calling for attention as he was trying to focus on something important.

Another defender along the wall shifted nervously and made a comment. "I've got a bad feeling about this." To which some of his comrades told him to shut up.

Then a flicker of a shadow caught Wilhelm's eye. And then another. Then all he could see were flickers of shadows moving amongst the forest past the tree line. "I think I see them," he said. As he concentrated more and more, he started to notice a low buzzing sound, like the sound of insects orchestrating their usual symphony, but it was different... unnerving.

What is that?

As if to answer Wilhelm's thoughts, Vell muttered, "It's the Scourge."

Wilhelm didn't believe he heard correctly at first. "What did you say, Vell?"

Vell borrowed a bow from a nearby defender and held it at the ready as he looked off into the distance.

Wilhelm repeated his question, and Vell responded. "It's the Scourge, Captain."

This sent chills down Wilhelm's spine. In fact, it already felt like he had a chill running down his spine when this very noticeable one decided to join in on the run too.

He looked around and realized that the defenders closest to him and Vell looked at him in wide-eye and slacked-jaw shock. They all silently screamed at Wilhelm asking him what to do.

"D-Defenders!" he yelled in a shaky voice, "Make ready!" His orders were echoed throughout the defensive line. The almost-coordinated sound of feet stomping and weapons clattering as people that were caught in their revelries and recumbency clamored to attention.

Only then, after the commotion had been made, did Wilhelm turn to Vell and ask if he was sure.

"I'm sure," Vell said. Then he nocked an arrow to the bow and aimed. Wilhelm looked to see where Vell was aiming and spotted something trying to inch out of the shadows of the forest.

"Is that a... fox?" Wilhelm wondered aloud.

But as soon as the words came out of his mouth, he knew something was wrong. The 'fox' inched forward into the light and was promptly hit with an arrow. Cheers of accolades went up. Regardless of what it was he hit, it was an amazing shot considering the distance.

"You're pretty handy with a bow too, eh, lad?" a defender with a heavy accent said to Vell.

Vell just nodded, and then he said, "There'll be more. Aim for the head or burn them completely."

Wilhelm was astonished.

"H-How... wh..." He did not know how to begin to ask the questions that flooded his mind like a torrent.

"I lost my memory when I was younger," Vell said, putting down the bow. "A traumatic event or something. But my mother told me that we had been on the run from the Scourge since the fall of the north." Vell turned to look at Wilhelm, almost eye-to-eye. "I'm sure, while on the run, we had to fight them."

It sounded ridiculous to Wilhelm, but yet possible at the same time. "So your body remembered?"

"That, and the hours of training I do each day," Vell said.

"What's going on?" a loud, angry voice came from below. The owner made his way up the stairs to the battlement, each foot pounding its presence into the ground with every step.

When the Commander finally reached the walkway at the top of the stairs, still taking his time to announce his presence and letting people know his temperament through his feet, he repeated his question, tone demanding a satisfactory answer.

Some of the nearby defenders muttered responses, but shut their mouths when the Commander screamed his question again.

"What! Is! Going! On!?"

Wilhelm closed his eyes to prevent a sigh from escaping his lips. He stepped up, and the Commander finally looked at him. "Commander, there was a report of activity in the tree line."

The Commander took a deep breath and straightened himself. "What sort of activity, Captain," he asked in a voice that obviously masqueraded as calm.

"The Scourge," Vell interrupted, half his attention elsewhere.

"Possibly the Scourge," Wilhelm said.

Both the Commander and the Sub-Commander, who was almost always in tow, looked at each other with eyes that almost looked like they would pop out of their sockets at any moment. They both turned back to the Captain. The Sub-Commander was the first to recover his voice and cognitive ability. "Are you sure?" he said, then continued, "What do we do?"

"It looked like some sort of fox or skinny dog," Wilhelm said. He then pointed across the field to where the tree line ended. "Vell shot it."

"Where?"

Wilhelm turned to look exactly where it was.

But he couldn't find it.

"It's gone!" one of the defenders yelled in disbelief.

A murmur went up. Everyone saw the shot, but no one saw what happened to the corpse.

"It was consumed," Vell said, still looking out in the distance.

The choice of words unsettled Wilhelm. "What do you mean?"

"It was dragged back and consume by the others," Vell said.

"You mean they eat their dead?" the Commander asked.

"Not really 'eat', but take in and... consume it..." Vell said. He obviously had a difficult time trying to find the words to explain it. "It... absorbs it? Makes it a part of itself? Something like that."

"And how are you so sure it is the Scourge?" the Commander asked. He started to sound irritated.

"I…" Vell paused. He glanced at Wilhelm, but then looked away when Wilhelm did not offer any help. "I don't remember."

"You don't remember?" the Commander said, his voice raised by the end of the question.

"Yes," Vell said, looking back out towards the field. "But this… this feels familiar."

The Commander did not like that. "Have you even seen the Scourge, boy?"

"Commander," the Sub-Commander whispered loudly to the Commander, "he's Instructor Keiara's son."

The Commander waved off the reminder, his irritation growing. "Yes, yes, I know."

Vell picked up the bow again and prepared an arrow. "Yes, I've seen the Scourge. Have you seen the Scourge?"

The Commander visibly bit back his anger and mumbled, "No, I haven't seen one."

"We were considered too young and too important to be on the front lines," the Sub-Commander said in an attempt to rescue their dignity.

"Well, there's one there," Vell said, nonchalantly, as he pointed his nose towards the field.

Everyone focused on the tree line, but it was easy to find the mark walking slowly out of the tree line, low to the ground.

The Commander gasped loudly. "It looks like an ugly… deformed f-fox!"

Vell let his arrow loose, and again it found its mark. The malformed, foxlike creature slumped on the ground.

"Wow, amazing shot, Vell," the Sub-Commander said. He couldn't help himself, despite the earlier exchange. Vell returned the compliment with a silent nod of thanks.

"Look! A group of them," a defender yelled.

Wilhelm turned his attention back to the field. In the small moment that his attention had been turned, a small group of deformed forest creatures, all the same color and texture, had made it to the fox's corpse. Wilhelm flung his head away from the sight and almost flung his lunch, when he witnessed a small, almost squirrel-like creature viciously biting a chunk out of the fox's head.

"They're eating it!" someone cried in horror. A gaggle of gurgles and vomits were heard along the line.

Vell nocked his arrows and let a few fly, one after the other. Not all found their mark. Of those that did, their victims were subjected to the same fate as the Scourge fox.

"They're feasting on each other!"

More and more nightmarish woodland creatures crept out and tried to get to the corpses of their fellow Scourge, or drag their bodies into the tree line and back into the shadows.

The Commander shook himself out of his catatonic state. "What are you doing!?" he asked to no one in particular. "Fire on them!"

"B-But sir, they're too far away," a defender said. "We would just be wasting arrows."

The Commander stepped well into the defender's comfort zone. "We have more than enough arrows. Just don't let them close in."

Wilhelm took up the cry. "Let them arrows loose," he said in a commanding voice. "Think of it as the live-fire target practice you've been asking for!"

Echoes of the command and affirmatives rang out across the line.

"What about the expedition teams?" Vell asked.

"Captain," the Commander called. "You keep watch here. The Sub-Commander and I will prepare the base and evacuate any non-essential personnel."

Wilhelm was worried about the expedition teams as well. They were the most experienced, but that would not mean much if they were surrounded and cut-off by the Scourge.

But to his credit, the Commander had heard Vell's concern as well, or it was already at the top of his mind. He turned to the Sub-Commander and said, "Your first task is to recall the expedition teams."

"We'll have to use the flares," the Sub-Commander responded, "and hope they see them."

"Repeat if necessary," the Commander said, "I think the entire forest knows we're here, so let's use the horns as well... at least the first few rounds."

"Affirmative, Commander," the Sub-Commander said, and then trotted off.

Maybe the Commander was not so incompetent after all, Wilhelm thought.

"Captain," the Commander said as he turned to Wilhelm. "We cannot lose this base. If we do, it'll be over for all of us, and especially those teams stuck outside the perimeter. Hold the line at all cost."

"Understood," Wilhelm said with a nod.

"Thank you, Captain," the Commander said before running off to organize the rest of the base.

Wilhelm turned to Vell.

"Vell," he said, "whatever happens, stay close to me, got it?" Vell nodded at Wilhelm before setting another arrow loose. "But run when I tell you to run."

Vell did not respond to that.

In the escalating fervor, Wilhelm did not know if the boy heard him and did not respond, or just did not hear him. It didn't matter to him – Wilhelm knew that he needed to do everything he could to keep his promise to Keiara.

11

The tension was palpable. Each step was carefully observed and measured before it was taken. And with each step, the eyes had to rescan its surroundings for signs of danger before repeating the agonizingly slow process again with the next step.

The forest was not as thick as it had first appeared from the base. More than enough light filtered down to the floor and allowed the mixed group of soldiers and mercenaries good visibility to scan for danger. As one of the foremost group in the expedition's formation, they needed to take each step seriously.

Thankfully, despite the lack of activity in the area over the past decade, a well-worn path still remained. This made it easier to carefully monitor each footstep before and after they were taken. When the tedious process is repeated enumerable times, each little moment can add up to a lot. But each member of the team took their steps seriously; the experienced mercenaries who could've acted like they had been there and done that, and the government soldiers who stereotypically had a disdain for soldiers of fortune. Instead, they were a cohesive unit. If their uniforms or outfits were similar, one could not tell them apart except, maybe, through age and scars.

But going at this pace all morning and into the early afternoon was grueling, and the signs were starting to show. Keiara knew a break was needed and she called it when they made it to the next clearing.

"Don't let your guard down though," Tilian said as Keiara announced the break. "We're in enemy territory, so keep an eye out."

The group settled down for a late lunch. Someone even built a small fire to warm their food and drinks. They sat together, surrounding the fire, fatigue slipping away as they regain their stamina and strength but eyes still watchful and volume still controlled. There was laughter and there were smiles, but there was also an acute awareness of themselves and the surroundings.

Keiara smiled, glad that at least some of the training had took.

"So, Instructor Keiara, what exactly *is* the Scourge?" a young soldier asked.

Keiara laughed. "You don't have to call me Instructor anymore," she said. "Your training is officially over."

"Don't spoil it for the rest of us, Keiara," Tilian said. "Soldier, you still have to call me Instructor Tilian because I'm still teaching you."

"Then you have to call me Instructor Keiara, Tilian, because I'm still teaching you," Keiara said with a smug look on her face.

Tilian laughed, almost a little too loudly. "Eh, I better let that go then, or I'll have to call you Instructor Keiara for the rest of my life."

The group laughed, but stifled it when it became too loud.

As some of the most experienced mercenaries, as well as one of the so-called leaders, it made strategic sense for Keiara and Tilian to be in different groups of the expeditionary force. However, Tilian was adamant about being in the same group as Keiara.

"At the very least, I know you have my back," he had said, "and I know you can handle whatever comes at my back."

The truth was, he was scared. But he was not going to show it, though he was going to make pretty darn sure that he gets a good chance to make it out alive. That was teaming up with his chosen and sometimes reluctant partner, Keiara.

"Sorry," the young soldier said, "it's just that we have ranks in the military, so someone we respect, like you, should have a rank too."

"Yeah, it is a little weird for us to see you guys not use ranks," another soldier said.

Keiara nodded. "It's understandable," she said. "The way I see it, we're in this together. And despite what we call each other, if we have respect, even if it is for one's skills, then it doesn't matter what rank we're called.

"But if you really feel you need to add something to my name, you can simply call me Ms. Keiara."

"Alright, until we come up with something better," one of the soldiers said with a laugh.

"Sounds good," the young soldier agreed. "Now, back to my question, Ms. Keiara: what exactly is the Scourge?"

Keiara looked up at the forest canopy in thought. *How do you answer that?*

"That's a tough one, lass," Tilian said to the young soldier.

It was a tough question. Keiara thought back to her training when she was a young girl. For her people, the Scourge was something that they had dealt with for generations. It was almost considered one of their duties to contain the threat. The technicalities of what Keiara was taught was way beyond what the normal people of the world could understand, and it would not help them at all.

What the soldier is really asking was how to identify the Scourge and how to deal with them.

So that is what she focused on in her explanation.

"Malformed creatures?" one of the soldiers asked after the explanation.

"Yes," Keiara said, "because of the way they absorb living things."

"Wait, so does that mean they can absorb plants a well? They are living things too, right?" a mercenary asked.

"They can, but they don't usually do that unless it benefits them or they are desperate," Keiara said.

"So do they think?" the young soldier asked. "You mentioned that they would do it if it benefits them. That means they have to choose, right?"

"Yes, they think, especially the bigger more complex ones," Keiara said. "In the beginning, at the very basic level, they are more instinct than thought, but that changes as they grow bigger and more complex. In that regard, they prefer to absorb more complex and thinking creatures…"

"… like people," a mercenary said with a gulp.

The rest of the group agreed with slow, thoughtless nods. Their minds tried to process what they just heard.

A sudden noise from down the path brought the squad's mind back to the present, and reminded them that they were in possible Scourge territory. Fortunately, it was another group from the expeditionary force.

"Hey, what's going on?" asked the lead mercenary.

Someone answered, saying something about lunch.

"Mind if we join you? We're waiting on some stragglers," the other team's leader asked.

"Sure," a soldier replied.

The squad leader shouted to his team and said that they were going to take a break here until the rest of the team caught up.

"You shouldn't' be separated like this," a mercenary from Keiara's group said.

The mercenary leader sighed. "I know, but those guys keep falling behind. They're supposed to be careful and all, but at this rate we won't ever get done."

"No need to rush, lad," Tilian said.

"Better safe than sorry," a soldier from the other squad agreed.

The squad leader sighed. "Sergeant, are those runners back yet?"

"Not yet, Instructor," the soldier replied.

"Damn it, I've already sent four guys back there," the squad leader said. Then he turned to the Sergeant. "Should we send another one? I don't want to send a pair again."

"Let's wait for a bit, Instructor," the soldier said.

"You have no idea how many breaks we've had today," the squad leader said to Keiara and Tilian.

With the breaks and the men you've left behind, your team still managed to catch up to ours? Keiara thought. She wanted to say something, but decided to keep it to herself for the moment. She turned to look at Tilian and saw him looking at her. Keiara shook her head slightly, and Tilian's face had a brief expression that was gone before anyone else noticed. It seemed that Tilian was thinking the same thing.

After an extended wait, the squad leader almost gave up. But just as he ordered his group to get up, a lone soldier came towards them, disoriented.

"Where have you been?" the squad leader yelled as he approached her.

"I-I," she stammered as she held a hand over her midsection and then brought another to her head. "T-The... the... "

This made Keiara suspicious.

"What's the matter with you?" the squad leader called as he and his group continued to walk towards the disoriented soldier.

"Stop!" Keiara yelled in a loud voice. She had already stood up, but now she had taken out her sword and stood in a defensive stance as well. "Don't move any closer."

"What are you talking about?" the squad leader turned around and said.

Tilian and the rest of Keiara's group stood in defensive positions as well. They weren't going to take the risk.

"Jumpy bunch," a mercenary from the other group said with a laugh.

"Don't approach her," Keiara said again, firmly. "She may be infected."

The disoriented soldier looked worried. She looked over herself, still clutching her gut, and started to cry.

"Oh shit," the squad leader said as it finally clicked. He stepped back and clumsily drew his sword. "W-What do we do?"

"Don't panic," Tilian said in a deep, reverberating voice. "Take a deep breath and observe her carefully."

"Why are you clutching your stomach?" Keiara asked the disoriented soldier.

"T-The..." she stammered, and then she started to sob.

"Hold your arms up," Keiara said. The soldier complied. Keiara moved her head at Tilian and indicated to him to visually inspect the girl. "Okay, now turn around, slowly," Keiara said.

"I-I ran as fast as I could, b-but I threw up," the girl final said. She held back her sobs as best as she could. "T-The f-foxes... they mauled him."

Keiara inched closer to the soldier as she inspected each bit of her. She did not look infected, and she did not have the telltale spots.

The soldier finally just fell to her knees and started sobbing again. Keiara reached her and patted her on the shoulder. "You left him alone?"

"No," she said, barely a whisper, "the others told me to run and get help."

"We have to hurry!" the squad leader said. "Come on, troops, let's go!"

"Wait!" Keiara yelled. "We can't rush into it."

"Like hell we can't," the squad leader said, and then he ran off. His squad followed, though reluctantly. The Sergeant nodded apologetically and asked Keiara's team to take care of the disoriented soldier. Then he left too.

"W-What do we do?" a soldier asked, signs of panic starting to spread.

Keiara turned to the female soldier and asked, "Are you okay?" The soldier still seemed out of it but managed a nod. Keiara helped the soldier up and then turned her attention to everyone else. "Alright, listen up. We cannot run off haphazard like the other team. We need to stick together. Now, grab your gear, don't worry about the fire, and let's get ready to move out."

"What about her?" a soldier asked.

"Yeah, won't she slow us down?" another asked.

"Then we will slow down," Keiara said. She turned to the girl, still supported in her arm. "Can you keep up?" The girl nodded, possibly afraid to be left behind alone.

"Let's go ladies and gentlemen," Tilian said to the team, and they scrambled to get the essentials together.

"Can you carry her?" Keiara asked Tilian.

The request caught him off-guard. "Carry her? Like a wee baby?"

"More like on your back," Keiara said.

"Aye, but I won't be able to fight very well," he said.

"I-I can keep up," the soldier interrupted. Her posture and facial expression did not convince Tilian and Keiara, but they had no choice.

"Okay, try to keep up, but let us know if you need to slow down," Keiara said. Then she pointed at two of her troops. "You two make sure she is okay, and help her a bit. But remember, you need to be ready to fight and be aware of your surroundings."

The two soldiers nodded.

"Alright, let's go," Keiara said. "Cautiously but quickly."

By the time they arrived, chaos had tumbled into more chaos.

"Stay back!" a soldier yelled.

A plea for help turned into a scream as a foxlike creature bit the soldier's exposed leg. Another creature, snout bloodied, bit the soldier closer to his torso.

The group from earlier had somehow found almost half of their squad separated by two of the fox creatures. Another pair of the creatures was behind the cut off soldiers grabbing and biting at a bloody heap of something. Cut off and surrounded.

"Those bloody fools," Tilian said under his breath.

They had obviously rushed in and allowed the more nimble Scourge to cut them off and separate the group. While the people panicked, the Scourge quickly (or sometimes slowly) devoured a target, and then another, which usually induced panic again. Even if the panic resulted in an attack, the Scourge could easily put them down and go back to devouring their initial prey.

And this was how so many lives were lost and soldiers were overrun by the Scourge.

"Keep together!" Keiara commanded her squad.

The squad tightened up their ranks, weapons facing outward. They left their backs exposed, but made sure to be very aware of it. The female soldier from the other squad joined in as she continued to follow the lead of Keiara's squad. The other squad took this as a cue to back off.

"Swords out. Move forward. Steady," Keiara said. Her squad followed the commands swiftly and as expected. The routine helped stay the nerves of the squad, but the nervousness was still present.

They walked steadily towards the first two fox creatures, eyeing them cautiously. As the soldiers stepped closer, the foxes lunged, but quick strikes by the troops kept them back. Slashing at anything would work with a normal opponent, but not the Scourge.

Eventually, Tilian pinned one down and stabbed it in the head. Two other soldiers took note of Tilian's actions and worked together to take down the second fox creature.

"Prepare a fire," Keiara called out to the other group, though she wasn't sure they would be able to reorient themselves and gather their wits enough to make a fire.

Cutting off or even cutting into the heads of the Scourge would stop them, but it was temporary. Somehow they reorganized themselves and, in worse case scenarios, would become multiple Scourge creatures that needed to be dealt with. You'd pray that they would fight amongst each other as a right to dominate the others, but often they were smart enough to take down the fresh prey before eating each other.

The members of the group that had been cut off now had a way to regroup with their teammates. However, they were in the process of trying to drag the fallen soldier before he became a bloody mess like his friend. Brave, but not a good idea.

"Move away," Keiara said to the helping soldiers. "Don't touch the Scourge, and especially don't touch the white splotches on his armor."

The soldiers complied, but one complained. "We have to help him!"

"We will," one of Keiara's soldiers replied.

But before they could make good on their word, they were interrupted.

"So, what kind of fire do you want?" the mercenary squad leader asked.

"The kind you burn the Scourge with!" Tilian roared.

The squad leader made a halfhearted reply and then rallied his troops to spread out and find kindling.

Damn it, don't spread out! Keiara yelled in her skull.

Nonetheless, she had to deal with the definite threat in front of her instead of the possible threats to another squad.

The Scourge foxes were well aware of the troops' presence, and made that fact known to them with a nasty snarl. Its friend decided to continue its feast while the former decided to dig its claws into fresh prey.

As usual, they would try to get enough to eat so that they can become stronger, Keiara thought.

"Same as before. Aim for the closest one. Forward!" she commanded.

They moved forward in unison, almost as a single, wide curve.

"Help, please." the fallen soldier pleaded before the Scourge sunk its claws into his body again and dug out another scream.

Sensing its doom, the creature tried to defend itself. But, like its fallen comrades, it was decapitated. And soon the fourth one fell too.

"T-Thank you," the fallen soldier said. "Now please help me up."

"Not yet," Keiara said. "We have to check you."

"Check me? For what?"

Keiara pointed to the splotches of dull-pink white on the legs of the soldier. "How'd you get those?"

Puzzled, the soldier explained that he and his dead friend had stumbled into a grass field. The field had some sort of mushrooms growing that released that when they were disturbed.

Keiara clicked her tongue.

"What is it," Tilian asked.

"It's those splotches. They are detectors for the Scourge. They can be tracked."

"W-Wait, so what do we do?" the soldier asked. His reprieve of relief was short lived.

"Take of your pants," Keiara said. "Shoes too."

"But I'll be running around naked," the soldier complained.

The expression that Keiara's face contorted into must've been horrifying to the fallen man, because he complied quickly when Keiara told him he'd either lose his pants or his legs.

Once they were off, Keiara took a torch to it and burnt off the spores. It unfortunately set fire to some of the fabric, but it was a small price to pay to save the armor.

Keiara then checked the soldier's legs. It was hard to tell if the Scourge had left its mark because of how pale he was. She did a quick flash through with the torch just in case. The soldier obviously did not like that.

The wounds the man received needed to be checked more thoroughly. Thankfully, it did not seem to have transferred.

With the adrenaline of the battle ebbing away, the members of Keiara's squad started to question her: was that the Scourge? She looked at them sorrowfully and nodded.

Keiara could see the looks in their eyes as each came to the slow realization of what just occurred – what they just faced. The traces of several different emotions flickered across their visage before they settled on one to keep. Keiara was proud to see that the units she and Tilian trained had chosen the right ones: bravery, determination, even satisfaction.

"What now, Ms. Keiara," one her troops said.

"Now," Keiara said as she stood up straighter and putting on an air of confidence, "we need to completely burn them before they wake up."

The troops exchanged nervous looks before Tilian barked. "Understood, Keiara." Then he turned to the troops and said, "Let's get to it, lads and lassies." He walked to the closest creature (or a part of it), carefully grabbed it, and put it into the fire. The action caused visible discomfort amongst the members of the second squad.

Tilian's display motivated the rest of his squad as well as some of the more clearheaded members of the second squad to bravely drag the corpses to the fire.

While most moved to quickly get the corpses to fire, the others just sat stunned.

"Keep the fire going," Tilian roared at the other members.

The mercenary squad leader almost fell backwards on his rear but somehow still had the guts to challenge Tilian. "W-Why should we do that? We need to return to base."

Tilian stopped cold. He slowly and dramatically turned to face the squad leader, his eyes wide like a mad man and a snarl that rivaled the one the Scourge made earlier. "Boy," he said in a manner that made anyone else feel small, "you best get your rear in gear or else."

"O-Or else what?" the squad leader dithered.

Tilian laughed a menacing laugh. "Else you're going to face true wrath, boy. One that even I wouldn't want to face."

And he was right.

Tilian made a dramatic show – to everyone – to look at Keiara's direction. And his instincts were right, Keiara was seething. It was the type of quiet fury that could lash out in an instant. And on someone as skilled as Keiara, that instant was more than enough time to draw a sword and slash off a head or two.

But the squad leader was stupid. Very obviously so.

He started to protest, but his fear started to melt away. "Her?"

He was about to start laughing before Keiara stepped towards him. In fact, she moved so swiftly that she was well within his personal space before one could finish a blink. And half an instant later, she had grabbed the boy by the collar and dragged him across the ground. He had been dragged quite a distance from the group before he even realized what had happened. He squirmed, but could not get free. He muttered curses and threats, but it stopped as he was lifted, one handed – armor, weapons and all – and his back was slammed into a large boulder.

The boy could not help but yelp.

"Now listen here," Keiara said. She could barely contain her fury. If she even thought of Vell being on the same battlefield as this idiot, her fury would be stoked to apocalyptic levels. She tried to brush that thought out of her mind. Tried very hard. "Enough with your damn posturing. We're not bullies here and we're not fighting normal people.

"How you became a trainer is beyond me. If you were a mercenary from our town, you'd be marked...no heralded as a disgrace.

"Now people make mistakes, and you have made mistakes that cost someone their life and almost cost half your squad their lives. Even a prideful man would have learnt from this by now, but you're showing pure incompetence and childishness here."

The boy started to protest, but Keiara's fist pounded into the solid rock near his head. His eyes would have almost bulged out of his skull if he hadn't closed his eyes so tightly. He might have even soiled himself if his entire body had not reflexively clenched.

Keiara leaned her face close to his. Under normal circumstances, having such a beautiful face this close would have been wonderful. It might have meant that there was a possibility that they were about to very, very lucky. But not in this case. It was the complete opposite. Keiara's demeanor reminded the boy of a bedwetting nightmare he had once been told. Now he was able to truly sympathize with the bed wetter.

"I am trying very hard to not imagine my son on the same battlefield as you even if it is not under your command. Your defiance in the face of your failure and incompetence is making it really, really difficult for me not to."

The boy gulped.

"Now you will follow my command or the big fellow's commands. You will not even pretend to have command of your squad anymore. You will watch us, and you will learn. And when you get back to base – if you get back to base – you will leave and you will never take a job with me and my mercenaries or my son again. Do you understand?"

The boy nodded, but Keiara was not convinced.

"Do not think that my appearance means I am a pushover. I have and I will kill people that put me, my family and my friends at risk. People like you who get people killed by being sloppy and stupid.

"So, do you understand?"

The boy nodded more convincingly.

"Are we clear?"

The boy noticed that Keiara's hand had somehow gone to a blade that was sheathed and nodded furiously.

Keiara dropped him from the boulder. The boy had not even noticed that he had been held up, feet dangling. He looked up at the boulder. He then saw the indentation and accompanying cracks Keiara's fist had made near his head.

As they walked back to the rest of the group, Keiara asked, "What's your name?"

"T-Terry, sir," he replied, not sure if it was a good idea for her to know his name.

"I'm Keiara," she said.

"I-I know," he said, then chided himself for it. "I mean, I know who you are."

"Then you can call me Ms. Keiara," she replied with a tight smile.

Before he could reply, a few loud bangs were heard high overhead.

"Damn it," Keiara muttered, then picked up the pace to the group. Most of them had their eyes to the sky.

"Did you guys see it?" Keiara asked when she and Terry got back.

"Yes," a soldier replied. "Three of them: red, green and blue."

Another set of flares went up, this time with an accompanying sequence of horns.

Tilian muttered and expletive.

Keiara turned to the troops. "Alright, I'm taking command here." She turned to the second group's sergeant. "Any objections, Sergeant?"

"No, sir," the Sergeant replied without even a glance at his old squad leader.

Keiara nodded. "Listen up," she announced to the group. "I'm Keiara, this is Tilian. We're in command, he's my second. We are in this together now. We'll temporarily be divided into 1st squad and 2nd squad, with 1st squad being mine and 2nd squad – that's you, Sergeant – being Tilian's.

"First, finish burning the Scourge here. Keep the fire hot enough to do so, but don't spread out. Make sure none of that stuff is stuck to your body, armor or weapons. It'll infect you, and it ain't pretty.

"Then we are going to move towards base, quickly but steadily. We need to be more aware of our surroundings than usual."

"What about our squad mate?" someone from 2nd squad asked, pointing to the mangled corpse.

Keiara sighed. "Sorry folks, we have to burn him too. Salvage what you can, but we need to burn him just in case he was infected but also so the Scourge doesn't absorb him if they come across him."

Then she continued laying out her orders. "We will move towards base, however if we hear of people in need of help, we will carefully identify and then move towards them. The more of us together, the more likely we all survive this."

"But that delays our escape to the base," someone said. Scattered signs of agreement showed that person was not alone.

"It does," Tilian said, "but what if you were on the other end? What if your friends were the ones that needed help?" Tilian pointed to the former squad member of 2nd squad. "What if we didn't help you just now?"

The guilt settled in as the silence echoed the words and images in the group's minds.

Terry was the first to move. He picked up his comrade, but it separated into a more manageable part, and he dragged it to the fire.

"Come on, we're wasting time here," Terry said, solemnly. Being the first to carry that piece of their former teammate was almost symbolic to Terry accepting responsibility.

"Why should we listen to you?" a member of 2nd squad said, tears in her eyes. "You were supposed to train us for this, instead you almost got us killed."

The Sergeant stepped in. "None of us took it seriously," he said with a sigh as he comforted the soldier. To the soldier's credit, she had held in her tears and held onto her brave face longer than expected. "Hell, we made fun of every other unit for being hard asses."

Keiara closed her eyes. She understood how a mercenary, used to the lack of structure, would have a challenge training soldiers used to rigid structure. Instead of pushing and being hated, it was easy to be the fun guy and be the one that everyone likes.

But in battle, that won't help anyone – the weak or the strong.

Another set of flares went up into the sky. All units needed to return to base. Base under attack.

"We need to head back to base, quick," someone said.

"We need to finish up here," Tilian said. People started moving, but others were not so sure.

"Why? If we take too much time, we won't make it to base."

"We all have a reason to rush back to base. My son is at the base right now," Keiara said. *Vell.* "But we cannot rush off because it decreases our chances of survival. This can be our fallback point if we cannot break through to the base. The Scourge hates fire."

There were scattered protests, but the group was generally in line. Those out of line were either hushed up, or they carried on with work anyways knowing that their protests about taking up time would take up time.

Keiara kept up a strong façade, but internally she kept battling her emotions and thoughts. She wanted to run to Vell.

Finally, they were ready to head out.

But then there was a far-off scream. Then more.

Another squad was in trouble.

Vell.

But Vell had to wait.

"Let's move," she said.

12

"Archers! Loose!"

The steady thrum of multiple bows setting loose their load could be heard. Then, a moment later, the scattered squeals of their prey as they are hit. However, it was eerily quiet compared to what one would have expected of the amount that had fallen.

And the cycle continued.

By now, the empty field in front of the base was no longer empty. It held a scattering of Scourge creatures, most looked disturbingly like diseased woodland creatures. The Scourge still was a distance away from the base's walls, but each foray brought the Scourge closer and closer.

Wilhelm carried batches of arrows up the wall to the defenders. He quickly distributed the ammo, and then surveyed the battlefield.

With each sacrifice, the Scourge either dragged the bodies back to be consumed, or they were used as distractions and cover for the Scourge to advance. With the brave actions of a few of the Scourge, others joined in, and slowly they scattered across the field. And if a corpse was left for too long, they would rise again; sometimes spawning another one from the corpses' dismembered part.

The defenders had to make sure both the corpses and the new entrants to the battle were cut down before they closed in on the base. It was still manageable, but eventually the defenders will have a hard time keeping track of all the activity on the battlefield and accurately attacking them.

Not to mention the need to open a pathway to allow the expedition teams to come back to base.

A few of the closer teams had already made it back in, but there were still a lot more out in the forest. The teams that came in had regrouped and were now helping to shore up the defenses. But not all of the teams came in unscathed. While fighting their way through, some of the teams almost did not make it past the Scourge.

Thank goodness for Vell.

His accuracy could pretty much be counted on, especially far range. He was able to help take down some of the Scourge and buy enough time for the teams to move out. Some were so desperate that they abandoned their gear so they could run faster and escape. But unfortunately, Vell couldn't help them all. At the range he was firing at, he could not risk firing too close to the incoming teams. Those that had to engage the Scourge in close quarters but failed could not be saved by Vell while they were still so far from base. All he could do was amplify the time that the fallen soldier's sacrifice bought the rest of the teammates as they could escaped.

Wilhelm tried to observe the boy and be sensitive to his condition. However, it was difficult, even under the best of circumstances, to see how he was doing. Wilhelm just hoped that Vell's stamina could hold out far longer than needed.

Although a few defenders throughout were tasked with firing fire arrows at the Scourge corpses, Vell was the one they could really count on to almost always hit the mark.

This, in addition to his other responsibilities and the normal stressors of a heightened situation like combat, kept Wilhelm worried about Vell's condition.

All of Vell's concentration was aimed out beyond the walls when Wilhelm approached him.

"Vell," he called as he took out some water and provisions he had brought up. "Let's take a quick break, shall we?"

"I'm okay, Captain," Vell replied without averting his eyes from the battlefield. Then he spotted prey, nocked an arrow, and let it loose.

"Just a quick one," Wilhelm said.

Vell turned to him, looked at Wilhelm's eyes, and then slowly nodded his head. "Okay, just for a bit."

They sat down, their backs against the wall, and shared the light meal. Vell closed his eyes as he ate silently.

The barks from both the Commander and the Sub-Commander echoed throughout the base.

"We need to hold this base, no matter what," the Commander yelled. "We cannot and *will not* fail!"

The Sub-Commander on the other hand was still orchestrating the retreat of non-essential personnel back to the fort behind the safety of the Wall. The problem was that the defenders were shorthanded and they needed support personnel to help them stay on base walls to defend. Some support personnel had decided to stay behind and help with the defenses. Noble if done right, but it was causing chaos in the evacuation.

Any rushed evacuation was messy. People rushed out, leaving things in disarray. People left behind had to figure out what was going on in the disarray. Critical tasks may need to be completed, but the personnel was nowhere to be found; either evacuated or somehow on the frontlines. Then messengers had to be sent around to people that definitely had the all-clear to evacuate, only to find that some of them want to stay to defend the base, and then multiple messengers end up conveying the same message to the same person. Yes, it bred chaos.

But the overall strategy was simple: get everyone who is not helping the defenses off the front lines, and continue to keep the defenses up as long as possible to do this.

And of course, bring the expedition teams back.

"How many teams came back in, Vell?" Wilhelm asked.

Vell slowly opened his eyes and blinked purposefully. Then he turned his head to look at Wilhelm. "I'm not sure, Captain."

Wilhelm scoffed. "You don't have to call me Captain. You can call me Wilhelm."

Vell look back out towards the rest of the base. "It makes me feel more..." he hesitated, "comfortable."

"Well, whatever makes you more comfortable, Mr. Vell," Wilhelm said with a laugh.

They continued eating in silence even as the world around was in chaos. It seemed to be a slow blur to Wilhelm, and the sounds felt like muffled distortions. The chaos around them relaxed Wilhelm. Maybe it was something he picked up with the time he spent with Vell.

But just then, screams pierced Wilhelm's tranquility, followed by a monstrous, deep roar that ripped through the air. Wilhelm was not sure if he stood up or if the roar made him jump up, but he found himself up and looking for the source.

"What was that?" someone along the defensive line said.

Someone in the distance could be heard yelling. They kept yelling and yelling.

"Team coming in!" yelled a defender. The line echoed the call.

After the Commander echoed the call, he turned his attention to the defenders of the gate below. "Gate team, get ready to open the gates."

But another bloodcurdling roar went up, much closer this time, accompanied by terrified shrieks.

"What the hell is that!?" a defender shouted.

"There! To the northwest – the edge!" another cry went up.

Wilhelm looked to the left, to the area that met the wall and the forest. The area was almost devoid of Scourge; surprising considering that it was one of the closest forest edges to the base. The right side of the base was closed off with a rocky terrain that filled out a divot in the Wall and forced the forest edge much further out. It was a good natural defense, which made this base an even easier point to defend. The area surrounding the base was kept almost empty of anything higher than a blade of grass to keep the sightlines clear. But the forest edge was thick and difficult to see into.

However, the creature that was roaring and stomping in the forest could clearly be seen.

"Bar the gate!" someone said.

"But the Commander said…"

"Bar the gate! Quick!" the Commander echoed the first person.

"What about the team coming in?" a defender asked.

"We can't risk that thing coming in here," the Commander roared for all to here. "It'll kill us all!"

The team outside the base barely kept themselves in front of the creature. There was no order, just panic, as the team ran as fast as they could away from the creature.

When the creature came closer, the size of it dawned on the defenders. It was the biggest Scourge creature that Wilhelm had ever seen. Humanoid in shape, but just barely, it stood about 12ft high, the same pale-white skin as its Scourge brethren, with a bulky figure that looked muscular but could have just been the deformities often found on the Scourge. It roared with a mouth full of jagged teeth, eyes yellow and red. In one of its hands, it held some sort of weapon. It was difficult to make out at first because of the distance and the way the creature swung the weapon. But then, as it came closer, Wilhelm's heart sunk. The weapon that the creature swung so deftly was not a weapon: it was a person.

"Open the gates! Open the gates!" one of the expeditionary team members said as he ran to the gate. Somehow he had run far ahead of his teammates.

"We can't," a defender yelled.

The man started cursing a storm and insulting everything from the ground to the sky. "Open it! You're going to get us killed!"

"We can't," someone said, "not until you kill that thing."

The man was incredulous. By now, two other members of his team arrived at the gate. Same response.

"There is no way we can kill that troll!" one of the soldiers screamed. She had stripped off most of her armor, and was just left with her uniform and weapon. The others at least had some of their armor still on, but she had totally forgone it. A good choice too, because she was less winded than the other two and was also one of the first to reach the gate. If the gates would open to let them in, stripping her gear down would've been a good tactic. But stuck outside having to face the giant… the troll, she might as well have been naked.

"Can't we open the gate quickly?" Wilhelm yelled. "Just enough to squeeze them through?"

"No, Captain," a gate defender yelled back from the ground. "We've already braced the gate. Taking it down and putting it back up would take too much time."

Someone yelled an expletive. Then a roar that sounded like it was aimed directly into their ears brought their attention back to the front. The troll was a lot closer now. The other members were trying to slow it down so that the gate could be opened. But it was almost useless. The troll stood as high as the gate itself, and only a few feet lower than the base of the battlements.

If that thing can jump, it'll be able to climb over the wall instead of having to go through the gate! Wilhelm realized.

At this distance, the gruesome weapon that the troll wielded could be clearly seen. By some miracle, the head was still attached, but the back bent in a weird way, and every time the troll used his weapon, the arms flapped all over the place.

The troll was close enough now that arrows easily found its mark. However, the arrows just embedded into the troll's body, none worse for the barrage. By now, more of the team had arrived at the gate. Unfortunately, they were boxed in – troll bearing down on them, gate locked behind them.

"Take it down!" came a faint cry from down the line.

"We can't watch them die!"

The troll ignored the pleas. It swung its weapon again at the team near the gate. One of the team members was caught unprepared and was knocked away. Thankfully he missed the spiked barricade and ended up in the open field, but that might not have mattered since his body no longer looked like it had life in it.

More arrows poured onto the troll, but it did not deter it. This distraction almost allowed the Scourge free-reign in the field.

"Archers! Don't forget the field," Wilhelm yelled. "Keep them back! Don't let the troll distract you from keeping the other creatures back!"

The troll flung his weapon again, but he was too close and his weapon smashed into the spiked barricades in front of the wall, impaling the dead weapon. The troll just roared again and swung its fists at someone near the gate. Whether it connected or not, Wilhelm could not see. All he heard was crunching and screaming accompanied by a discombobulating roar.

A mercenary and another soldier somehow had lagged behind and found themselves behind the troll, with the open field to their backs. They did not use it as an opportunity to run however. Instead, they used it to taunt the troll to attack them so that the rest of their teammates could get out from between the gate and the troll.

"Come on, you ugly bastard!" the mercenary said. He had a spear-like object, maybe a stick with a weapon crudely attached to the tip. He stuck the troll from behind and quickly yanked out the shoddy spear. The soldier took his cue and stuck his proper polearm into the troll as soon as the mercenary took his out. They backed off after a round or two of this, but the troll barely registered the provocation.

"Come on!"

The mercenary and the soldier rammed the troll again, together this time. The times where the troll did not respond had lulled them into reacting slower than they had been, and this time it was an error. The troll turned around and smashed the mercenary across the neck and upper abdomen, sending him flying across the field. The soldier lucked out and was only thrown aside while the troll focused on the polearm instead.

Some of the team members trapped at the gate took the opportunity to run, but some were not fast enough and the troll, in a rage, used its shoulder to butt against the gate in an attempt to pin the fleeing soldiers. It worked. Someone had been caught.

Now its attention turned outwards towards the people who had escaped from the troll.

"What are you doing, kid?" a soldier next to Wilhelm said. Wilhelm looked towards the voice and was shocked to see that Vell had jumped on top of the battlement's parapet and looked ready to leap below.

"What are you doing, Vell?"

"I need to stop that troll," Vell said. His focus was intently on the battle below.

"But that's a long fall!" Wilhelm said. "You'll be injured."

"I can't promise that I won't," Vell said. A nearby roar caused Wilhelm's focus to shift for a second. "Get the gate ready to open when you see a chance." Wilhelm turned around and Vell was gone.

"Vell!" Wilhelm yelled as he ran to look over the wall. But as he reached the wall and looked over, he was greeted with a roar right to his face. The roar was different; a piercing roar, without the deep, guttural properties of the earlier roars. It was a roar of pain.

Somehow Vell had managed to jump off the wall and land on the troll's back, embedding his sword deep into the troll. The force of the blow sent the troll staggering forward as the troll roared and tried to grab the boy with its right hand.

Vell then pulled the sword out with his right hand in one quick movement and used the momentum of the maneuver to transition into a wide spin that lopped off the troll's hand. The way Vell had swung, and the way the hand had been flung made it look like Vell was fighting slightly-melted cheese.

Still in mid-air, Vell swung again and took off another portion of the troll's arm before landing.

Wilhelm suddenly remembered what Vell had said and turned to the soldier next to him. "Tell the gate team to get ready to open the gate when we give the signal." To his credit, the soldier did not just simply yell the command off the top of the wall. He took his job seriously and ran all the way down to tell the gate team in person.

Wilhelm turned back to see the fight, both to look for a good opportunity to let the troops back in as well as to witness the amazing fight firsthand.

He was just in time to see Vell run towards and angry troll, sidestep a feeble attack, and slash the troll across the right of its torso. The sweeping motion carried him behind the troll where he was able to slash the back of its leg, sending the troll to its knees.

The expeditionary team, at least the ones that were conscious, took the opportunity to gather their courage and circle the troll from the front. Once on its knees, the soldiers started jabbing the troll, tepidly at first but with more fury the more they stabbed.

From the back, Vell continued his attacks to keep the troll down. Then he bounded up the back of the troll and stood above it head with his sword in both hands, blade pointed down. Vell then drove the sword into the troll's neck, where the spine would have met the skull if they had bones. The troll was further disoriented by the move, but it did not die yet.

Without the go-ahead from Wilhelm or Vell, the base gates opened and a stream of soldiers came out to help put down the troll. Some made their way past the troll to help gather the fallen comrades.

With the troll disoriented, and it being attacked from both the front and the back, Vell could concentrate on the important thing: cutting off its head. He took his sword in one hand and chopped, and chopped, and chopped like a butcher cleaving with a dull blade. But each swing was powerful, so it was not long before the troll's head flopped down in defeat and fell off while Vell stood high on its back in triumph.

A cheer went up all along the lines: a small victorious reprieve in a tiresome battle. Even the Scourge looked reluctant to move forward. But they were still out there.

"Great work, ladies and gentlemen! But don't forget, there are other Scourge out there to take care of," Wilhelm yelled.

The Commander loudly agreed to the sentiment before adding his orders to continue shooting.

Wilhelm went down to greet the incoming team personally, as well as Vell. He reached the open gate and saw the troll sitting on the ground. From this angle, it looked even more terrifying. Its body was so massive that it almost blocked the entire gate. Wilhelm stood there with a mixture of awe and fear momentarily capturing his attention.

A round of cheers snapped Wilhelm out of it.

For the first time in a while, he saw Vell grinning. Sure, it looked like it was trying to hide, but the joy inside or the accolades outside could not keep the grin off his face no matter how hard Vell tried. The troll killed, and the last of that team walking back in, there was reason to be happy, even if Vell's mother was still out there, along with more than ten other groups.

"Great job, Vell," Wilhelm said.

"Thanks, Captain," he replied.

But the cheering and accolades suddenly turned into gasps and yells.

"What the hell?"

A hand, a normal sized one, emerged from the body of the troll and tried to reach out for Vell. Vell, instead of running or killing it, just stood there and looked at it. The hand could not reach Vell, but Wilhelm could not believe that Vell had not reacted. Then without warning, the hand lunged out even further and caused Vell and the others to step back. What was more terrifying was a head, solid and wrapped in that pale-white Scourge skin except for a gapping maw where a person's mouth would've been, had emerged, along with a portion of their torso. The head started moaning and groaning, the noise not making any sense. Suddenly, the mercenary who was with the expeditionary group that just came in stabbed the head with his sword, cutting off the last words.

Help me.

"W-What was that?" the mercenary asked.

"Probably someone who was absorbed by the Scourge," Vell answered nonchalantly.

"A-Absorbed?" the mercenary said. He looked back at the vague likeness of a person again and covered his mouth as his gut roiled in protest.

The Commander had come down to see the valiant act, or what remained of it. But before he could say anything, Vell said, "Commander, be sure to burn the troll completely. Fuel oil will help."

"Uh, sure," The Commander said, slightly off-balance. He quickly regained his composure. "Magnificent work by the way, Vell." He turned to the troops and said, "You heard him! Burn it before it spawns."

Vell continued back up to the top of the base wall, only pausing to accept a container of fresh water from a supporter. Wilhelm caught up with him, but so did the mercenary that stood up to the troll.

"Hey, Vell, what did you mean when you said that it was someone that was absorbed?" the mercenary said.

Vell took a long drink from the container. He let out a satisfied sigh before he explained. "The Scourge absorbs or devours living things, like animals or people. That's how it grows, by consuming them and making them a part of itself."

The mercenary visibly shuddered. "Thanks for saving my bacon, Vell. I wouldn't want to end up like that."

"I'm glad you made it out alive, Bernard," Vell said. "I'm not sure Mira would spar with me anymore if she knew I let you and your team die."

"Nah, she'd still spar with you, but she might accidentally kill you," Bernard the mercenary said. "But not much of my team left. The group that came in with me was actually what is left of two teams."

"Oh…" Vell said, resigned.

Wilhelm on the other hand was shocked. "What happened to the others?"

"We went to help another team, but that monster… the troll… took too many of our guys down. That's when a group decided to hold the troll back as long as possible to give the rest a chance to run."

"But that troll was right behind you," Wilhelm said.

"Exactly," Bernard said, leaving the important bits unsaid but understood.

Sadness almost overcame Wilhelm. But he managed to control himself and gathered it into a deep sigh. He remembered that there were still teams out there. Wilhelm looked up at Vell and realized that Vell's mother was still out there.

"How come that thing came out of the troll and reached out to you?" Bernard asked Vell.

They had reached the battlements and could see the battlefield again. Thanks to the shock of the troll's defeat, the battlefield had not changed very much. The Scourge creatures were not nearly as brave as they had been earlier when they had rushed across the field separating the forest and the base. However, that grating sense of unease continued. Sometimes it intensified and it felt to Wilhelm like it was crawling down his spine and his nerves making his body and muscles reluctant to move.

Vell paused for a moment. He had picked up a bow and some arrows. "I don't know," he finally said, and then he nocked an arrow and let loose.

"Is there a way to get people out?" Wilhelm asked, but suddenly felt stupid for asking something so obvious, like a hopeful child.

"You have to purify them, but I don't remember how. My mother knows though," Vell answered.

"You mean I killed someone that we could've saved?" Bernard said in astonished disbelief. "I-I just saw a creature reaching for you and I had to act!"

"It's not easy to save them," Vell said.

"How did you mother figure it out?" Wilhelm asked.

"She…" Vell paused again, lost in thought.

Or so Wilhelm thought.

The feeling of unease had suddenly vanished. It felt like the entire area was silent, almost deathly so. Wilhelm looked around to see if he was the only one that sensed it, but he also caught Bernard looking around. They both locked eyes, wary and unsure, then they looked back out over the base. Things seemed to move slowly and people seemed disoriented. It was like they were all trying to listen to a soft whisper that was carried by the wind.

A chill went down Wilhelm's spine. Not the same type of sensation as the uneasiness of battling the Scourge. It was from a real chill in the air. Though the air slightly bristled, it seemed like the air had become frigidly cold. It confused Wilhelm because he could see the warmth and feel it, but somehow his body had thought he was cold. It was like there was an absence of something. Something missing.

Then Wilhelm realized: the chittering and noise from the forest had stopped.

Why would the Scourge stop making noise?

"There's something coming," Vell answered, as if he had heard Wilhelm's thoughts.

He looked around. The stillness betrayed the given answer, but Wilhelm believed Vell and started to look at the stillness as the calm before the storm. The uneasiness threatened to choke him. His mind screamed at him, telling him to run, to panic, to get out of there.

Fear.

Vell suddenly turned to the base and yelled off the top of the wall. "Get ready! To arms!"

The crowd was stunned. It was uncharacteristic for Vell to yell like this. Did the victory over the troll get to his head?

"What are you doing? Get ready for combat!" he yelled again. He then took up his bow and picked up three arrows in one hand, each separated by his fingers, and somehow nocked and loosed them in succession into the tree line. Each arrow was in flight longer than Vell had taken to nock and loose them. He shot another volley, and then stopped. He put his head down for a long moment. Wilhelm could see him shiver a bit. But then he looked back up with a different set of eyes – the calmness was beset with fury.

"I-I'll get you more arrows," Bernard said.

"No," Vell replied. His voice had a different edge to it. "You and your team just came in. Rest, and then get some proper weapons and gear."

"Why?" Bernard asked, the gulp of nervousness he intended to hide was too obvious.

"Because it is about to get busy."

"I'll get the arrows," Wilhelm offered.

Vell had nocked another arrow, but he managed a nod of appreciation to the Captain.

The Commander stomped over to the base of the inner wall and screamed up at Vell. "What do you think you're doing, boy?" he said, both arms held at his waist in a threatening manner. "You may have killed the troll, but don't let it get to your head! I'm in command!" He held his angry stance for an awkwardly long time, but Vell was not swayed. The Commander finally gave up his intimidating pose and was about to stomp his way up to the battlement's walkway again when an earthshattering roar boomed across the terrain and reverberated through everyone's bodies.

The roar caught the Commander in midstride and sent him sliding down the stairs. It would have been an embarrassing moment, if it weren't for the fact that the roar had terrified all of them. This roar was nothing compared to the troll's roar from earlier – this was something much, much bigger.

The silence that followed was just as deafening as the roar itself. Everyone just stood, wondering what to do, waiting for the next roar, waiting for… something.

"What are you doing? Move!" someone said. It was the Sub-Commander. He moved through the crowds, shoving and pushing, in hopes of awakening the masses from their bewilderment as he made his way to the Commander.

As he helped the Commander up, another roar penetrated the atmosphere. Wilhelm swore that he felt the wall shake. It sounded much closer and much fiercer.

To this answered another roar. Not the one that shook the earth or knocked the Commander off his feet. The roar was a primal one of rage, a challenge to the other creature that he will not be moved. It was a roar that came from deep within Vell.

Wilhelm realized that his stupor was not helping, and neither was everyone else's stupor. He shook off the peacefulness of inactivity. "G-Get ready! Wake up! Get ready for battle!"

Bernard rushed down off the walkway to his teammates and ushered them off to get geared up. Scattered echoes resounded the call to get ready, though the mood was still uncertain.

Then the chittering from the forest started. It built up in intensity and volume to a level not heard of before. The noise hit a fevered frenzy, a raucous that almost seemed like… joy, like a cheer of victory. It ate into Wilhelm's spine and caused his muscles to lock up.

"What the hell is t-this?" he stammered. He almost bit his tongue saying the sentence.

And then Vell roared again, but out at the enemies surrounding the base, hiding in the forest. The roar's intensity seemed to match the cacophony from the Scourge.

And it silenced them.

Or so it seemed to Wilhelm.

"Archers, get ready!" Vell yelled to the base defenders. "Defenders, prepare to hold the line!"

The Commander didn't protest this time. He was shell-shocked. But he would not have had the chance to protest anyway, because the creature roared again.

The challenge had been accepted.

The Scourge moved out of the tree line, the smaller animals first, then the slightly bigger ones.

Some of them even combined together so it looked like the smaller animals were riding or clinging on to the larger animals.

The base responded with a scattering of arrows: most missed their shots.

The demented forest creatures continued their march forward in coordinated fashion – nothing like the earlier skirmishes. Those that came across their fallen brethren on the field stopped to nibble on them or push them forward as a sort of defensive shield.

The closer the Scourge got, the more accurate the base's arrows became. But in the time it took for the Scourge to march forward and the defenders to get their heads on straight, much bigger creatures started coming out of the forest. Some were recognizable, even if Wilhelm had only seen them in books and pictures, but others were beyond recognition as if they refused to hide their true nature behind the forms of weak creatures.

The Commander regained his senses. "Shoot the Scourge! Burn them, shoot them," he yelled. "We *cannot* let this base fall! Defend it at all cost!"

Those words sounded like fighting words, but Wilhelm's emotions were not easily swayed by mere words. He wondered if the Commander's desire to hold the base was so that the expeditionary teams could come back, or for his desire for glory on the battlefield.

It didn't matter to him. He was going to fight as long as he could.

By now, the barrage on the Scourge looked like a hail of black streaks falling from the sky. Even arrows shot out halfheartedly ended up hitting something. More archers focused on blanketing the field with fire arrows, hoping to prevent the Scourge from going forward.

It worked.

The intensity of the barrage and the fire that swept across the battlefield, either on Scourge corpses or on the fields of grass, had created barriers that the Scourge had trouble going through. However, Wilhelm wondered if any of the expeditionary teams had made it to the field, only to be stopped by the same barriers that stopped the Scourge.

The Commander yelled out in triumph as the hordes scurried away from the fires. He took it as a sign that they were retreating.

"Good work, troops!" he yelled. "Keep it up!"

Wilhelm thought the celebration was premature. The Scourge was still out there, and so were the expeditionary teams. What was more worrisome was the creature that had made that earthshattering roar. Was it one of those creatures that had trotted out? Or was it something bigger and more terrifying?

"Down!" Vell said as he grabbed Wilhelm and the soldier next to him and pulled them down behind parapets.

Wilhelm wasn't sure what had happened. He saw a flicker of movement before Vell pulled him down. But the whole battlefield was full of movement.

A gurgling scream came from somewhere down the line. Another scream accompanied by a yell for help rose up shortly after.

Vell peeked over the wall. He looked around, eyes shifting, but quickly pulled his head back. Another cry rang out, along with disconcertion along the line. By now, some of the soldiers had taken a cue from Vell and had hesitatingly ducked behind the wall. A brave, or maybe unwary, few continued their scattered attacks with their bows.

"What's wrong, Vell," a soldier asked.

"They're shooting at us," Vell answered.

Wilhelm could hear it. Scattered thuds or knocks on the wall; a ping or a ding on a metallic object; or a dash along a stony surface. It sounded like heavy raindrops. The sky had gradually darkened and the wind had cooled, so naturally, Wilhelm thought the sounds signaled the start of a rain shower.

But it was a different type of shower.

Men and women could be heard screaming along the line, some even in the base below. It was already too late by the time someone thought to call incoming.

"Incoming!" rang out a yell. Then the call was picked up across the walkway and the base. But there were already casualties. A soldier had a part of his head blown off right next to Wilhelm. The soldier looked puzzled, and his mouth still moved, even though he had a big portion of his face missing. Wilhelm saw it in detail as the man toppled off the top of the wall and landed with a crunch in the base.

Wilhelm felt a thud on the other side of the wall he clung onto. The reinforced wall that he had put his faith in suddenly felt very insufficient.

Then the sky darkened, like a rain cloud had suddenly cast its shadow over the insects below. A curtain of whitish-grey blobs filled the sky. It was surreal to Wilhelm. It looked like they hung in the air, frozen, but then the illusion broke and it showered the base and its defenders with death and explosions of fear.

Troops caught in the open were torn apart. Bits of red and white flew all over the place and splattered onto the first surface they found. Sometimes the surface was a wall or the ground, but more often than not it was another screaming patron of the carnage. Soldiers in full gear were knocked unconscious or their bones broke and shattered, if they were lucky. Those that weren't had chunks of their bodies gouged out by the projectiles, or they gave a much gentler touch and just pierced the soldiers enough to lodge into their flesh.

The support staff that had stayed behind to help did not stand a chance. Trained in the fine arts of making the living quarters less unpleasant to live in and the food less unappealing to the senses, many were torn to shreds for their lack of armor and combat training. Wilhelm saw a young boy clutching an arm because his arm had been severed. Unfortunately, the arm was too long to have been his. A young lady, one of the support members recruited from the surrounding areas to help with laundry, had been struck several times and somehow ended up nailed high against a wall. She was still alive, but her body was so mangled that it was a miracle she was not screaming in pain.

The terrifying screams and moans scattered across the yard, coupled with the ringing in Wilhelm's ears from the thunderous impact of the projectiles, left Wilhelm's senses numb and null. His eyes lost focus, and the world looked like a flood of red and grey, speckled with bits of white. He stood up, exposing the upper part of his body above the wall and surveyed the destruction. Screams mixed into a dull throb in his head. He found blood on his hands and wondered if it was his.

His mind numb, he knew he had to do something to get the ringing out of his head and his head out of the fog. He remembered they were shooting arrows for some reason, so he picked up his bow and searched for ammo. He fell to his knees as he felt his way amongst the red and disturbances on the ground. All he needed was an arrow. He felt a rush of wind above him, and he thought he heard someone whistle his name. Whistle his name? How would that work? But his hand continued to search among the entrails for arrows. He finally found one, but a piece of meat was stuck on it. He waved it off, and then finally flicked off the meat. He nocked his arrow and stood up, turned to the forest, and shot his load lazily. He had looked down at the last second and saw his finger against the arrow. He realized that the piece of meat on wrapped around the arrow was not meat but a finger.

Wilhelm lost his balance and crumpled to his knees. He could not hold his head together. He could not hold his thoughts in one place. His body roiled and roiled for some reason. He felt the burning in his throat. He tried to swallow it back, but it just made him choke and cough. And then his body heaved again, finally releasing his precious lunch all over the ground.

The only thought that came to his mind was that the color looked different now. And then his stomach complained that it was empty. But for some reason he wanted a simple piece of bread or some vegetables. His mind did not seem to like the idea of a nice, meaty meal.

Another round of explosions and thuds reverberated through the ground. It did not bother Wilhelm, for some reason. It felt soothing, like the rocking of a wagon with a comfortable bed of linens to lie on. His eyes closed. He wanted to keep them open, but he just felt so… comfortable.

And then a hand grabbed him. And another. Then they hoisted him up.

"Get up, Captain," a familiar voice said.

"Is he in shock?" another asked.

"Maybe, but he's definitely not hurt," the first voice answered.

Wilhelm was put down in a sitting position, back against something solid. He felt wet and tired. His mind wandered and he wondered about the last time he showered. He looked at his hands and wondered what it would be like to shower in wine. But then he started to get annoyed. Some incessant bother kept antagonizing him. He wanted to wave them off but only mustered a mumble.

"Captain, are you okay?" someone said. Wilhelm had trouble remembering his name, but knew he was a mercenary. "Captain!"

The annoying sounds grew louder and louder. His nose started to smell a strange mix of odors. His mind started to wonder what they were. He reflexively tried to sniff more, but his body rejected it and he started coughing and gagging. Someone patted him on the back.

"Make sure he's okay," a voice said.

"Wait," another said, "where are you going?"

"I need to help with the line."

Wilhelm remembered something about Vell. "I-I need to find Vell. I promised his mother that I'd bring him home."

"Calm down, Captain," someone said. "Vell is fine."

Someone came to them and asked, "Is he hurt?"

"No, but we think he's in shock."

All Wilhelm could think about was finding Vell and getting him out of there. He just had to fight this fog in his mind.

"What's going on here?" a voice roared. "Is the Captain asleep on the job?"

"No, Commander, he's in shock."

The Commander laughed. "I knew it," he said and the chortled. "The wonderful battlefield, a chance for glory, and here he sits like a child." He laughed again as he walked away and started to bark commands.

Wilhelm wanted to get up. He needed to get up. He needed to find Vell and get out of here.

Somehow his minders read his mind and helped him stand up. The fog was slowly clearing, but he felt sick to his stomach, and he felt dizzy.

"Here, drink this," a female voice said and offered a container of water.

"T-Thanks," Wilhelm managed to mutter. His senses seemed to be clearing although his body wanted to revolt against it. He drank more of the water and his body could not resist the deluge. He kept drinking and drinking until the container could not present any more of its contents.

Then his body heaved again. He tried to hold it down, but it roiled yet again. He let it go. And from deep within, a loud belch let out. The smell of guts mixed with the aroma of his leftover lunch had overpowered him and he had to shake his head at the stench. But then when his sense cleared, he wished he hadn't been so quick to dismiss his stinky breath. The smell of blood, guts and feces made him want to puke. Thankfully he had already puked and his body did not heave like it had earlier.

"Captain?" his minder said tepidly.

"I'm up, I'm up," Wilhelm said. He shook his head again and then slapped himself in the face with his free hand. He looked at his minders and recognition came to his mind quickly. "Thank you, Bernard. And you, uh…"

"Private Zoe," the girl said. "I-I was trapped at the gate earlier with the troll."

"Part of the other team that we tried to help," Bernard added.

"I see," Wilhelm said. "Are you okay?"

"Physically, I'm fine…" she said before an almost imperceptible moment of distress flashed across her face. She looked down as if to hide it. And even after a few moments had passed, she did not finish her sentence.

"I understand," Wilhelm said.

He turned his attention back to the battle. He looked up at the top of the wall to the battlements. Too many corpses dangled over the edge. Too much blood dripped down the wall. But the archers still continued, making sure to duck behind the parapets as needed. Wilhelm witnessed the tactic's successes, as well as a few failures. But the barrage coming into the base had subsided. The bad news was that the outgoing barrage had subsided as well.

"They're pushing through!" a voice yelled out.

"Oil to the walls, now!" someone else yelled.

A group formed up in the yard behind the base's gate. The Sub-Commander walked by and gave the command to form up and prepare for a breach.

"Damn, they're almost to the wall," Bernard said. He turned to Private Zoe and said, "Gather as many of the walking wounded and get them out of here. Organize teams of survivors if you have to." Private Zoe nodded and left.

"You should do that too, Bernard," Wilhelm said.

"What about you, Captain?" Bernard replied.

The sounds of battle closed in. Panic screams along the wall called out for oil, rocks, anything.

"They are rushing the walls!" a soldier yelled out.

"Damn it, I have to get to Vell," Wilhelm said. His strength returned and he went up the base's wall to look for Vell. But as soon as he reached the top, he saw the state of the battlefield.

The Scourge had made their way forward. He could see the little creatures that used their tails to fling the barbs of white Scourge flesh at the defenses. The fire had spread but was subdued and was not concentrated enough in any area to hold the Scourge back. Creatures had died putting them out, corpses piled on top of smoldering remains. For the glory of the Scourge, apparently.

But the disturbing thing was that the remainders rushed the spiked barriers. Some were swift and bounded up only to be, thankfully, shot down by the defenders. However, others had run so hard and fast that they impaled themselves against the spikes. They did not seem to care. Their bodies continued to flail, their mouths continued to grab and eat any piece of flesh that came within reach – whether Scourge or that of a defender. The bigger creatures closed in, several of them looked like the troll that had almost killed Bernard's team. There were other creatures, just as big. One had a long pipe hanging off its face with big, floppy wings coming out of its head from each side, its body the size of three wagons. Each of its steps shook the ground. It used the long pipe on its face to pick up smaller Scourge creatures and fling it towards the base. Some flew at the wall, some at the defenders, and some even flew into the base.

It was absolute chaos.

The oil bearers finally reached the top and they dropped hot oil on the Scourge clogging up the spike barriers. The screams and screeches were sickening.

Another genius had splashed fuel oil out over the top of the wall and onto the Scourge in front. Then they lit the liquid on fire. This managed to delay and even bring down some of the bigger ones, but it was a danger to the integrity of the wall. Even though it was reinforced, the core was still wood.

A gleeful, almost insane, cackle rang out through the base. It was the Commander. He was shouting all sorts of slogans and idioms about the glory of battle.

"It's a good day to die, troopers!"

"We'll take more of them down to the graves than they will!"

"No victory without sacrifice!"

And of course, "The base must not fall! Defend it at all cost!"

All bullshit.

This battle, the Scourge, the chaos, the deaths... there was no glory in this. Just a sliver of a chance of survival.

"Breach, breach!"

Somehow a big one had crushed the gate. The whole wall rattled when it broke, as if the weight of the Scourge pouring onto the defenses had strained the integrity of the wall. And, now, with the gates shattered, the integrity had been compromised.

"They're using the dead as ramps!"

Wilhelm turned to look out over the wall again. His face would have been taken off by a Scourge attacker had it not been for an attentive soldier. Wilhelm silently thanked the soldier, and the soldier nodded with a smile just before another Scourge creature appeared and attacked the soldier. Wilhelm tried to help, but didn't have the chance to. Another bash to the wall made it tremble again, sending Wilhelm off-balance. Then another Scourge climbed up, and bit into Wilhelm's armored shoulder. Wilhelm instinctively slammed his shoulder into the wall and bashed the Scourge's body. When it fell off, Bernard came from behind and stabbed the creature in the head before flinging it off the wall and into the field.

Somehow, the Scourge had flung enough of their brethren into the spikes to pile up and make a convenient ramp up to the top of the wall. The flood was no longer restricted to just the gateway. The waves of creatures were going to overwhelm everything.

As if it wasn't already terrifying enough, the earthshattering roar rang out once again. Almost as a reply, the intensity and volume of the Scourge attacks increased.

"Incoming!"

Another wave of the Scourge projectiles flew into the base, hitting friend and foe alike.

"They don't care if they hit their allies!" Bernard screamed at Wilhelm as they recovered from the barrage. Another Scourge jumped up over the wall, and Bernard worked with Wilhelm to quickly take it down before another appeared.

Brave men and women continue to bring oil through the chaos to the defenders still up on the wall. But it was getting more and more difficult to maneuver within the base with the combat thick and heavy.

The Commander had gone into the thick of things. He was on the ground in the base, yelling and screaming, with an ecstatic grin on his face. He was reveling in his first real foray into the deadly art of war. And he looked the part too.

"Come on, troops!" he screamed, waving his sword high in the air. "Push them out! We can defeat them."

His second-in-command, the Sub-Commander was right there with him. Their expressions gleamed; it looked like a hero and his sidekick. Both seemed to be capable fighters, which surprised Wilhelm. But he did not have time to marvel at the captivating scene of the battle – he had to find Vell.

"Incoming!" the cry came again. Wilhelm knew he should appreciate it, but he was starting to get annoyed. He almost continued his slow journey across the battlements to find Vell.

But thankfully, Bernard did not take the call for granted.

"Oh crap! It's a big one, Captain," Bernard called. "Get down. Get down!"

Wilhelm obeyed and ducked down.

Bernard was right. It was a big one.

The projectiles rammed into the wall. Individually, they sounded like a piece of hail slamming into the roof. Together, it sounded like the world was falling apart.

Then there were the projectiles that were launched at a higher arc and fell like polearms thrown from heaven. Those fell into the base and pierced anything in its way. It did not matter if it were living or dead, friend or foe – it decimated all it touched.

Too many soldiers and people fell. The good news was that the Scourge were hit as well.

"What is this madness!?" Wilhelm yelled. He grabbed an armored piece of... something... to protect the exposed parts of his body as he hugged the wall. But hugging the wall was another type of horror as the projectiles continued to blast the other side.

His fears were realized. With his head so close to the wall, he heard it starting to crack. The assault had its effect.

"How is the Scourge using our tactics against us?" Bernard screamed. "I thought they were just mindless predators."

Wilhelm didn't know. Hell, he didn't even realize that they had used their tactics against them. But it was so simple once he made the connection: they were using the barrage to keep us from attacking and to kill us from a distance.

"T-That takes thinking," Wilhelm said aloud.

Bernard laughed a sort of laugh that someone makes when they have half given up. "Now that's scary," he quipped sarcastically.

"But they're so brutal," Wilhelm said. "These creatures that were so ready to eat each other when they fell, how can they suddenly fight and sacrifice themselves, even get shot at by their own allies, for... for what? Victory?"

All Bernard could do was manage a shrug before they heard more cracking along the walls.

Cries rang out.

"We can't hold the wall!"

"We're going to be overrun!"

"Off the walls! Off the walls!"

Wilhelm literally saw soldiers leap off the walls, from more than ten feet high, and land on the ground. Some of them landed in something that broke their fall, others did not do so well. Chaos surrounded Wilhelm and Bernard as troops fought their way, Scourge or each other, to get to the stairs and ladders and off the wall.

"What are you doing!" the Commander yelled. "Get back on the wall and defend!" He kept on screaming and screaming, even going as far as kicking soldiers who had jumped down and were still rolling on the ground in pain. "Get up there, you cowards! This base cannot fall!"

The battle had reached a lull on account of the earlier barrage. People slowly recovered, but the chaos from the wall caused confusion down in the yard. Screams continued to echo, both from the injured and the terrified.

"I said get back up there!" the Commander yelled again. "This base cannot fall. *I* will not let it fall!"

And this was the worst moment for another barrage to happen.

There was no one left on the wall to cry out for incoming. The chaos had caused the troops to cluster together as they fought to find cover and to defend themselves. And the fading light of the day made it harder to see the details.

Another roar rang out, but it was drowned out by the chaos of the base. A few of the troops still clung to the wall, looking patiently for a chance to get off. This included Wilhelm and Bernard. These were the lucky ones. However, when the survivors remembered this scene in the future, the nightmares and the torment that followed would make them feel like their dead comrades were the lucky ones.

The projectiles rained down. It was so thick that it seemed to look like an avalanche of hard, dirty snow falling from a looming mountain. The screams of its victims were muted as it tried to escape the torrent as well. Men and women blew apart, their body parts mixed together as they flew up from the impact, only to be shot down again by the consequent deluge. It held a weird visual display to those who, somehow, were able to calmly look at the gruesome show before them. The bodies rippled and vibrated up above the ground and then were brought back down before repeating the cycle, as if a layer of pink and grey floated just above the soil. The rain of death caused the background to disappear and to look like dark paper for a flickering canvas.

Even when the show was over, the image remained so strongly in the audience's mind that they weren't sure if it was really over. The murmur and noise after the torrent felt like the ringing in one's ears after being blasted by a loud, sustained sound. It had a surreal, comforting quality to it that amplified the feeling of numbness in the audience.

Wilhelm had witnessed something else. The Commander was one of the first ones to receive the rain of death from above, however his trusty sidekick, the Sub-Commander, had pushed him away and taken the deadly gift from the Scourge in the Commander's place. Now, in the quiet aftermath, he could hear the Sub-Commander's dying words from afar.

"T-Thank you, Commander Lytton, f-for... everything."

The Commander held the dead Sub-Commander in his arms as he sat on the ground in disbelief. "Sub-Commander?" he said, shaking the body. "Sub-Commander!?" Each successive call rose in volume and in pitch until the Commander was screaming. "Sub-Commander Mayne!? Mayne! Mayne!?"

The cries of the crowd continued to rise in pitch and volume as well. More people than expected had somehow survived. But the vision before Wilhelm looked more like a giant monster had puked out the half-digested meat mixed with off-colored grains of Scourge porridge it had held in its stomach.

Bernard started to dry-heave next to Wilhelm. However Wilhelm had already regurgitated his lunch, and could not regurgitate anything more, even if his body wanted to.

The wailing continued, but Wilhelm's focus was on the Commander's. For the first time, Wilhelm personally witnessed how much love and affection the Commander had for his friend. Without regard to decorum or manners, the Commander wept and wailed like a delirious widow who had just lost the love of her life. It was both a touching and heart-wrenching scene to witness.

The Commander looked around, lost, as his wailing subsided to a sob. Questions were on the tip of his tongue as he muttered incoherently. Was the war over? What happened? But none of the questions materialized as he looked around dazed and confused. He hugged his friend closer for a moment before trying to get up.

But the battle had not ended, let alone the war.

Scourge started to walk through the exposed gateway. It was hard to tell if they were walking menacingly slow or cautiously slow. Whatever the method, the truth of the matter was there: the Scourge had not been defeated.

Just as the first set of Scourge creatures found their prey – people or even their fallen comrades – Vell appeared and started the attack.

He swung his sword swiftly, cutting off the head of a creature in one swing, then moving almost instantaneously to another. Vell's swings looked wide and wasteful, but they were efficient in both movement and use of energy.

His attacks gave the survivors a chance to recover. The ones closer to the gateway started to get up and stand their ground. Some started to drag incapacitated survivors out of the way and to towards the Wall. Soldiers who survived on battlements came down slowly as they checked their surroundings. Wilhelm and Bernard formed up with Vell and started giving the invading Scourge some pause.

Groups of men and women stood up. Most were hurt, but the ones who could move and fight on their own stood up. Others helped by dragging themselves out of the way or helping others. Slowly, groups came together and started to hold their defensive lines.

The Scourge still trickled in, almost as if to give a chance for the fighters to practice on them before the bigger creatures came in.

A smile appeared on Wilhelm's face. He caught Bernard's eye, and the smile spread to his face as well. It was a chance to fight back, maybe to turn this battle around.

But it wasn't meant to be.

"R-R… Retreat!" a voice screamed, piercing the silence. The solidarity of the survivors would not have allowed a mere voice of cowardice to break their resolve.

Except this was not a mere voice.

It was the Commander.

"R-Retreat!" he screamed again.

The survivors looked at each other, not sure what to do. Those that had gathered up to fight were too close to the front now to turn tail and run. Not only would they leave the wounded and incapacitated to the Scourge, but they would most likely be taken down as well.

"All is lost! Retreat!" the Commander screamed. He sounded delirious. Scared. But it was his actions that sealed the deal.

The Commander started running towards the Wall. He continued to push, shove, and even drag people towards the Wall. All the while, he continued to call for a retreat. He yelled that all was lost. He yelled that it was over.

As if he changed his mind, he turned back towards the front lines and ran back.

Maybe his courage had come back.

No, it did not.

He had run back to grab the body of his friend, and drag him towards the Wall. Apparently he could abandon everything and everyone to the Scourge, but not his friend.

It was a slow, stunned reaction. People did not move. Fusses were not made.

Silence.

But that changed when the earthshattering roar cried out again. This time, it was much closer.

The Commander's voice was no longer the lone voice that echoed throughout the base. Panicked screams picked up the call for retreat as people dropped whatever they were holding and rushed to the Wall.

Even though the gate at the Wall was large, the scramble of people caused it to become clogged with panicked bodies. Those that were too weak or unfortunate found themselves on the ground, praying not to be trampled by the stampede.

On the frontline, another sort of stampede threatened to overwhelm the confused defenders. The roar had somehow given the Scourge more courage and they started to enter the base at a much quicker pace. The scattered groups of men and women who had been brave enough to stand back up and back on the frontlines after the devastating attack were now rattled by both the panicked call for retreat and the renewed intensity of the Scourge.

Wilhelm debated an organized retreat as well, but was reluctant to abandon those that were too slow or unconscious and could not retreat without help. But Vell charged into the Scourge lines with a roar and made Wilhelm's decision for him.

Vell screamed with fury, his eyes no longer displaying the control over his emotions as it had before. This wild and uncontrolled Vell was a stark contrast to the picture of Vell that Wilhelm had built in his mind.

"Hold the line!" Wilhelm yelled.

The troops around him still seemed uncertain of what to do.

"Hold the line!" Wilhelm repeated. "We need to hold the line so people can retreat." Wilhelm wasn't sure anyone wanted to sacrifice themselves to let others run. His words were both to encourage everyone and as a statement that he declared so he could not run from it.

"HOO-AH!" Bernard grunted as he beat his chest in military fashion. A few scattered grunts answer Bernard's. Bernard, not satisfied with the response, repeated the grunt. "HOO-AH!!" The response was louder. Bernard repeated it again, and again, and again until it was all the remnants could say and think except for how to take down their foe.

"Hoo-ah," Wilhelm said. He looked at Bernard and Bernard grinned at him.

"It's a good day to die, Captain," Bernard said.

"As good as any," Wilhelm replied. "But it would be a better day if we live."

Bernard nodded, then he turned his head to the others. "We're not going to let Vell do all the work for us, are we?" he yelled. The reply was a resounding 'no'.

"Stay with your groups, but don't stray too far from the others!" another mercenary called out – a survivor from one of the expeditionary teams. "Don't let them surround you and don't rush to take on too many. They'll overwhelm you."

As the mercenary said that, Wilhelm realized that Vell had been hacking and slashing through the Scourge lines and had gone deeper into them. He was now surrounded.

"Damn it!" Wilhelm said between his teeth. "Vell!"

But his worry was unwarranted. It was almost like Vell had wanted to be surrounded. Now he could go wild without the worry of hitting a friendly. And the sight of him going wild looked almost like a masterpiece. None of Vell's sparring sessions had shown the type of furious grace that was on display here. It was almost like a passionate dance, but Wilhelm knew that it was not passion for the art that drove Vell.

Vell's pace was fast. His blades seemed to leave an after-trail that looked like he was waving ribbons instead of swinging swords. And he had no fear. Vell attacked the Scourge with whatever and however he was able to. He even sometimes used the Scourge against themselves, either as a weapon or as a springboard to amplify his momentum giving his blades more energy so they could glide into the flesh of the Scourge and out the other side. His awareness of his environment was beyond anything that Wilhelm had seen.

The teams approached the killing of the Scourge in a more conservative manner. They were positioned in a defensive circle, weapons facing out and backs inwards, to allow them 360 degrees of vision and attack. Each attack was made with a quick jab or slice by someone, followed by another from the person next to them. The set continued as needed. If they had to spin to engage or move to avoid, then another soldier will contribute. This made them masters of their sectors and reduced their need to concentrate on more than one area, freeing their minds to focus on survival. This was a tactic that was honed and developed over the years with the blood of the fallen and tears of the survivors.

Wilhelm made an angry stab at a Scourge creature, a wolf-looking thing, and it almost broke his rhythm. But the fact of the matter was that his government's military had no idea that this tactic existed even though it had thrown so many lives away in the war against the Scourge. They had to find out about it from a so-called band of selfish, money-hungry mercenaries. Wilhelm made a stab at another enemy, but this time Bernard quickly helped finish it off. One thing that Wilhelm was thankful for was whoever decided to use the mercenaries as a way to train the inexperienced replacement army that had replenished itself over the years of peace.

The defense continued, the mind dulled, the rhythm monotonous, but slowly and surely, the Scourge were kept from advancing past the base walls. Vell and his fanciful swordsmanship had kept the gate to the base clear of the Scourge. Any who made it through over the ramps were quickly taken down, either from range or when they entered the yard. Victory seemed close.

But Wilhelm knew that the Scourge would not stay away. They were endless, tireless, relentless. The volunteers who stayed were starting to show signs of fatigue. Even with rests between bouts as they rotated their groups from front to back, like a ring of groups of dancers dancing round and round so that each had a chance to be the one in front of the stage, Wilhelm knew that they could not outlast the Scourge. In a battle of attrition, the Scourge would always win.

Wilhelm called the groups' attention while they continued their fight. "Select those that are less experienced or need a break and rotate them out," he said. "Have them start taking the survivors who could not retreat, and get them to the Wall, inside the gate."

The groups cautiously reshuffled so that the volunteers could help the incapacitated survivors to retreat.

"Don't stray too far!" someone yelled. "Be careful of the Scourge."

Wilhelm's plan was to have the volunteers try to evacuate as many of the incapacitated people as possible. Then he would evaluate to see if they needed to evacuate or if they could hold out longer and wait for the expeditionary teams to arrive. He knew that if the fort commander back on the fort's side knew that Wilhelm was still alive, that there were people alive, he would keep the gates open as long as possible.

If they retreated, it would mean that the Wall would be sealed, and that the expeditionary teams would be on their own until the Wall was reopened.

Wilhelm had to hold out as long as possible. Vell would not be able to forgive him if he did not.

"Vell," Wilhelm called. "Vell!"

He chanced a departure from his group, but they wouldn't let that happen. As Wilhelm moved towards Vell at the gateway, the group moved together.

"Vell, there is a lull in the battle, so take a break," Wilhelm said. But Vell's back remained to him. "Vell," he said and reached out his hand to Vell's shoulder. Vell was shivering. "Are you okay?"

Vell turned with tears in his eyes. He was clearly not okay.

"It's alright, Vell, let's take a break," Bernard said. "We'll watch the gate."

"Those cowards," Vell muttered with a sob, "they ran away."

"Don't worry Vell, we'll hold them off for as long as we can," Wilhelm assured. He reached out and grabbed Vell, but he did not move. Then Wilhelm hugged Vell where he stood, and Vell broke into tears. It was tears of sorrow and sadness at first, but it turned into anguish and frustration. He held onto Wilhelm's body tightly, not because he did not want Wilhelm to leave but because he needed to grip something in his anguish.

Wilhelm continued to hold him for a long time.

Long enough for a most of the incapacitated to be removed from the battlefield.

One of the groups approached Wilhelm and caught his attention. "We think we've got most of the people back to the Wall," the soldier said. "We're going to pull back and rest."

Wilhelm wasn't sure what to make of the news. Were they abandoning the base? It made sense, but they were leaving teams out there.

"Captain," the soldier said with a pat on Wilhelm's shoulder, "we survived."

He didn't want to abandon them, even if there was a good chance they were dead. The memories of that battle long ago during the war flashed across his mind's eye. A pang of regret hit his chest. He had already been forced to abandon people before. He did not want to do it again.

But before he could say anything, Vell lashed out.

"We are not leaving! We have to hold this base for the teams to come in!" he yelled, spit flying out of his mouth and his eyes look like they were on fire. "My mother is still out there! Your friends are still out there! Your comrades are still out there! And you want to leave?" He was huffing and puffing at this point, his tear-filled, bloodshot eyes looked insane, and it scared the people in the group who delivered the news.

The person just sputtered and couldn't form a response.

"Don't be a coward, like that stupid Commander," Vell said. "You already stood and fought. Don't poison your courage with cowardice! Finish it, till the end!"

Wilhelm was not sure if the people were offended or not. It did not look like the group knew either.

Vell could not hold back anymore. He yelled. Then he roared. Then he cried, and eventually they all mixed together to form a guttural, primal wail as Vell dropped to his knees. All the words he yelled no longer made sense. It was like a dangerous beast... no, monster... that had been unleashed from the depths within Vell.

But it was deeper than that. His scream shook Wilhelm to his core, penetrated his nerves, and shook his body like his body instinctively feared it.

It was then that he realized that it was not just him that shook; the very atmosphere seemed to vibrate and resonate with Vell's rage. Then the earth shook, and the sky broke out with loud strikes of thunder exploding right above them.

Wilhelm looked up and saw it.

No, it wasn't thunder.

It was a roar.

Right above them was a creature so large that it hid the sky. The tail that whipped across the terrain was as thick as the walkway on the battlements. Its wings created a tempest even as it hovered leisurely above the base.

It roared again, the roar pointed up to the heavens above the flying creature.

Vell was still screaming, but he made a sound that almost felt like an answer to the roar above.

And then the creature dropped its large body down, destroying most of what was left of the base, save for the defensive wall. The creature's head could now be clearly seen as it whipped around looking for its prey.

It was a dragon.

A myth from fairytales and children's stories.

A dragon.

No, not just a dragon.

It was a Scourge dragon.

Wilhelm's breath caught in his throat. His body kept pumping breath through some other orifice in his body because he couldn't stop breathing, but he could not force his body to control it. Somehow bypassing the breath stuck in his throat, his body caused him to breathe rapidly. He was hyperventilating. He could feel the fear in his face as the tears threatened to flow and blur his vision. Maybe that would be a blessing in disguise.

The dragon had plenty of choices, but it was looking for something. Someone.

The lucky groups that were near the Wall ran towards the safety of the tunnel. The groups that were near its snout broke and ran while the dragon searched. Those that did not move were somehow ignored.

It was searching.

And then Vell roared again.

And the dragon locked eyes in Wilhelm's direction.

Terrified, Wilhelm almost lost control of all his muscles – all of them. His life suddenly felt so small and insignificant. His mind contemplated the mysteries of his world, and his life, as he lost himself in the dragon's deep, red eyes.

To be eaten by a dragon.

Better than a squirrel, he thought wryly. The thought made him chuckle out loud.

And the dragon almost looked like it was smiling.

Wilhelm gripped his sword. Somehow senses had returned to him, even if it was for a fleeting second. He had been called a coward all his life for abandoning his friends during the war. He knew the truth. He was commanded to watch from afar, then he was commanded to hold out as long as possible, and then his friends jumped to a glorious death and left him… they left *him*.

And their last command to him was to live.

But what was the life he had lived? He had always regretted following the last command. He should have fought to the very end with his friends. The more he thought about it, the more an evil thought set foot in his mind: did they jump into battle, to their deaths, because they were brave or was it because they were scared… scared to live?

Wilhelm gritted his teeth. It may be the end of him, but he was going to charge forward. He was going to run into a hopeless battle, and he was going to fight as long as he could so that the brave men and women next to him could live... live and fight another day.

His muscles flexed, his stance ready...

But it was too late.

Someone else had already run forward.

Vell.

Vell roared as he ran towards the dragon, sword in both hands. The dragon stomped its feet from side to side, like a toddler's happy dance. It did not care that each stomp sent buildings tumbling. It did not care that it crushed men, women or Scourge under its feet. It was locked onto Vell like and excited child, and then it roared.

The shockwave was enough to blow people off their feet, but its breath was the real power and threw people against any surface still standing.

Wilhelm had the wind knocked out of him. He could not see or hear anything as he tried to stand up. He knew he was shouting, yelling, but he could not hear anything coming out of his mouth.

He clutched... something, and used it to prop himself up. His vision slowly came back into focus. He slowly remembered Vell. Even as good as Vell was, he could not take a Scourge dragon alone.

The dull ache in his ears continued. His sense of sound limited to muffles and grunts. His tears filled his eyes at the thought of Vell being crushed.

Wilhelm did not want to see someone like that die, so promising a person. And Wilhelm did not want to fail to keep the promise he made to Vell's mother. But he needed to see. He needed to be brave enough to see it for himself. So he wiped his eyes and cleared his vision.

Then he saw it: Vell's back as he stood in front of the dragon – no weapon in hand – just clutching his hand near his chest. Something was in it, glowing.

Wilhelm rubbed his eyes again. He tried to focus, but he could not. His vision seemed to glow white, like staring straight into the sun on the most brilliant of days. He could see the dragon. It roared, Wilhelm knew, even though he could not hear it. It roared again.

And then it lunged forward, at Vell, towards where Wilhelm stood.

The glow intensified and filled his vision.

And one last thought crossed Wilhelm's mind.

Is this what death feels like?

13

"That's better, Elliana, but don't let your guard down."

It had been awkward at first, but Elliana had gotten used to wearing training gear. It almost felt like she had rebelled against the 'good girl' expectations, except that her mother and father seemed overly excited that she was trying something new.

The thought made Elliana smile...

... And lose her grip on her buckler.

Tatiana, seeing her chance, smacked the buckler and watched as one side flopped uselessly to the side.

"I told you, Don't. Let. Your. Guard. Down!" their instructor roared.

Tatiana laughed and started to make fun of Elliana.

But she let her guard down too, and Elliana had learnt a few tricks over the past few months. So Elliana exploited her friend's distraction and took revenge. She smacked Tatiana's leg with her wooden training sword and then hit Tatiana's sword from her hand.

This, of course, sent their instructor, Mira, into a rage. She had become better at holding in her anger and being more patient, but there was only so much one could change in just a few, short months.

Mira took up her instructor's sword – made of a different type of wood than the normal training swords – and started smacking the ground as she walked menacingly to the two young trainees. Once she reached striking distance of Elliana and Tatiana, the ground was no longer the target.

"Ow, ow!" Tatiana said as she tried to defend herself without her sword. "Stopp!"

Elliana giggled, even though each hit seemed like a whip striking through her training armor.

"Will you guys take this seriously!?" Mira yelled.

Due to her injuries, Mira had been forced to stay behind while the majority of the guild went to Fort Holden for the training mission. She complained every day that she was left behind with the old folks and children.

It was true that the old guild members came to the guildhall to drink and nag more than find mercenary work. And the children she was referring to were the trainees, too green to go on any real mission. Some, like Elliana and Tatiana, weren't even registered mercenaries so they couldn't take those types of jobs from the guild.

"I'm like a glorified babysitter!" Mira yelled again, finally stopping her attacks.

But thanks to the glorified babysitter, Elliana was having the time of her life. Who knew that a girl like her would find sparring and combat so enjoyable? She laughed again, which promptly earned her another smack and a barely-withheld grin from her instructor.

Mira sighed. "Are you girls going to take this seriously?" she said with a smile.

"Hey, I'm here because I'm bored," Tatiana retorted. "I just followed Elliana."

Mira turned to look at Elliana.

Elliana grinned sheepishly. "Have we ever taken this seriously?"

"Ugh!" Mira said, as she threw her sword across the room in mock-annoyance. It timed itself with the door to the training room opening, and an unfortunate man stepping into the room.

Luckily, the man somehow ducked behind the door in time and avoided the sword.

"Oops, sorry, but that's what you get for entering a training room without warning," Mira said.

"Apologies," the man said.

He did not look like someone that belonged to the guild. And he did not look like someone who frequented a place like the guild.

The man walked into the room and stiffly said, "Pardon the interruption, but you need to see the guildmaster."

Mira made a dramatic, shocked gesture. "Me?" she said, in fake-surprise. "Well, if that old geezer wants to bother me he can very well come here on his own."

The man looked flustered.

I guess he's not used to Mira, Elliana thought.

The man coughed into his hand, as a way to reorient his thoughts. And then he tried again. "I'm sorry, Ms. Mira, but the guildmaster is not able to come of his own accord."

Mira's eyes twitched, and she became serious. "What do you mean?" When the man seemed reluctant to answer, she yelled, "Out with it!"

The man lost his composure for a split moment and sputtered, "The guildmaster is bed, recovering."

"What!?" Mira said. "What is he recovering from?"

The man became increasingly nervous. He looked to both Elliana and Tatiana in turn, but they offered no way out.

"Damn it, if you don't stop stalling…" Mira said, as she approached the man. He was taller and even broader than Mira, but it did matter when he withered as she took a giant step in his direction.

"H-He fainted!" the man said, putting his arm up to protect his face.

The color drained from Mira's face.

She stood there for a moment before she returned to reality.

"Come on, girls," Mira said. Then to the man she said, "Out of my way. Where is he?"

"This way."

By the time they arrived, the guildmaster was sitting up. He smiled as Mira and her two trainees entered the room. However, it was clear to anyone that the smile was an effort to cover the pain.

After the pleasantries, the people helping the guildmaster left the room.

"How are you, guildmaster?" Mira said, softly.

"I'm… I'm fine," he said with a smile.

Mira shook her head, but continued in a soft voice. "No, no you're not. What happened? Are you ill?"

The guildmaster glanced behind Mira, to Elliana and Tatiana. "Not in front of the young ones," he said.

"Look at you, calling them 'young ones'," Mira said, but she was clearly disturbed. She looked back at Tatiana and Elliana, and they took the hint. They bid their farewells and left the room.

Once the door was closed, Tatiana scoffed. "What was that about?" she said.

But Elliana was truly concerned. The guildmaster was so old that something like a fainting spell could turn into something serious.

Tatiana read her face. She frowned. "You think it's that serious, Elliana?"

Elliana nodded.

Tatiana sat down in a chair outside the room.

"His face did not look good at all," Elliana said.

"Yeah, more than usual anyway," Tatiana said, trying to lighten the atmosphere.

Elliana couldn't help but chuckle as she chided her friend for the remark.

She leaned against the wall, next to the door, and patiently waited. She could hear muffled voices occasionally, but never what was said. Her mind wandered and found her amazed at the fact that rooms could hide their sounds so well. Her home was not as quiet as it was here. Even Ms. Keiara and Vell's house was quiet.

She had been taking more of the responsibilities of keeping their house in order on her mother's behalf. With a huge portion of the town out on the mission, the remaining residents spent more time helping each other with the upkeep.

It was nice to be part of a town that helps each other, despite how big it had grown over the years. Elliana could not imagine it any differently now.

And helping to maintain Ms. Keiara and Vell's house helped her to connect with that community, instead of just being an observer.

But seeing the other side of Vell's life, the one she hardly saw, was interesting – at the same time, it was creepy. It was like she was spying on a private portion of his life. She fully became aware of it when curiosity caused her to wonder what it was like to lie in Vell's bed. She was tired, and she would clean the sheets anyways. But then her mother found her, curled up and drooling on Vell's pillow and buried under his sheets.

That was embarrassing, she thought with a smile.

She quickly glanced at Tatiana to see if she had caught her smiling to herself. But Tatiana was lost in her own thoughts, a signature pout appeared on her lips as her eyes glazed over as she focused on something beyond this world.

The wait was not a long one, only because the guildmaster and Mira were disturbed. The people from before, as well as some of the regulars of the guildhall made their way back in. It almost seemed rude, even though it was under the guise of concern for the guildmaster's health. The small moment that Elliana had observed as the door was opened showed a bit of annoyance at the intrusion. However, Elliana did not have the chance to observe any further as Mira rushed out of the room, head down, and walked off.

Tatiana, startled by the action for some reason, looked at Elliana and she took it as a sign to follow Mira. Mira was quiet the entire way, as they made it back to the training room they had been using.

The soundproofing in these rooms was phenomenal, more so than the other rooms, like the one the guildmaster met Mira in.

And as soon as the Mira and the girls stepped into the room, she took full advantage of the soundproofing.

Mira picked up a wooden training sword, a proper one this time, held it high above her head with two hands on the hilt and swung it down with enough power for Elliana and Tatiana to feel the wind of it. At first, her swings were accompanied by the usual grunts of exertion, but it quickly took on a whole new quality and turned into a raging tantrum that Elliana and Tatiana had never seen from Mira before.

Mira grunted in exertion, sweat streaming off her face and body, as she continued to swing the sword. Her form had lost its sharpness, and it was like a child swinging a stick wildly. Eventually Mira just threw the sword against the wall and crumpled to the ground.

"Mira!" Tatiana yelled as she rushed over to where Mira sat, on her knees, with a look of defeat.

"What's wrong, Mira?" Elliana said, scared to approach for fear of another outburst.

Mira just put her hands to her face and her body heaved, quietly.

Tatiana took a step back, and looked at Elliana for help. Elliana approached carefully. As she drew closer, she finally realized what had stunned Tatiana. Mira, strong, fearless, crass, and oftentimes lewd Mira was... crying.

And Tatiana hated crying.

She didn't know what to do with the emotion.

And now, the strongest person she knew, next to Ms. Keiara, was... crying.

"Elliana!" she whispered. Then she pointed at Mira and made a strange face. She mouthed the words 'Do something about this!'.

Elliana gulped and approached Mira. She put her hand on Mira's shoulder and asked, "Are you okay?"

It was a long while before Mira could answer. Finally, she shook her head 'no' as the words that tried to come out of her mouth blubbered into audible sounds of sobs. Eventually though, an intelligible word came out of her lips. "T-The guildmaster..."

But she could not continue.

Elliana looked at Tatiana. Tatiana's mouth hung open in shock.

"T-The guildmaster is going to die?!" Tatiana sputtered out suddenly.

Elliana gave her a look, but Tatiana did not get the hint. It was too late anyways.

Surprisingly, Mira nodded.

Tatiana and Elliana were shocked. They did not know how to feel. He had always been there, ever since they were little kids.

But then Mira shook her head.

That confused Elliana and Tatiana.

"N-no, he's not..." Mira started to say softly, but then she stood up suddenly and yelled, "Yes, Yes he is going to die!" She sounded too excited by that statement.

"W-What do you mean," Elliana said meekly.

"I'm going to kill the old man, either slowly or quickly, with my own hands!" she yelled, tears flew from her face as she made the declaration.

"So does that mean he's not dying?" Tatiana asked.

"No, he's not," Mira yelled again, but towards the wall. "He just fainted because of the... of the..."

Her shoulders shrugged again. "I'm sorry girls, I know I shouldn't cry... but I can't help it," she continued in a more solemn voice. Then she put her hands to her face again and continued crying. Muffled, she said, "I can't help it... I'm a girl too!" She continued sobbing. "No, not just a girl... I'm a person too. I can't help it at times. There is only so-so long someone can pretend to be strong for."

Elliana was worried. What was Mira saying?

Tatiana wanted to say something, but before she could, Mira looked up towards the wall she faced, slapped both sides of her own cheeks – hard – and then turned to look at the girls with a determined face, even as the tears continued to run and her facial muscles continued to spasm.

"I-I'm sorry for my weakness, girls," she said.

Elliana did not think, she just blurted out, "It's not weakness to cry or feel sad." Reflexively, Elliana brought her hand to her mouth. "Sorry," she said timidly.

Mira smiled. Then she forced out a laugh. "You're right, it's not a weakness to cry or be sad." Then she smiled again. A forced one, but a smile nonetheless. "Thank you, Elliana."

She cleared her throat and continued. "The guildmaster informed me that there is news from the Wall," she said.

Elliana's heart sunk.

"T-There isn't a lot of details at the m-moment, but," Mira tried to finish her sentence bravely but kept choking back her words. "T-The... damn it!

There were casualties... a lot of them." Mira's face contorted badly as she tried to control it with all she had. "A lot of the troops, government forces and mercenaries, were killed."

Elliana's hurt sunk further, dragging her body down to the floor. First, to her knees, then her head hit the floor as she bowed forward.

No! No! No! her mind screamed over and over again.

Tatiana fell back on her bottom. Her eyes looked beyond the walls around her. She just sat, stunned. Then the tears rolled down her cheeks. Confused, she wondered what they were as she wiped them away frantically. Then she focused back to the moment and steeled herself.

"M-My father?" she asked in a strong, but shaky voice.

Mira shook her head. "Sorry, we have no idea."

Tatiana's eyes glazed over again. This time, when the tears came, she let them roll down her face. She sat still for a long time, like a doll.

Elliana had to ask. She looked up at Mira, and asked about Vell and Ms. Keiara. Mira just shook her head and said the same thing. Elliana simply sunk to the floor and cried. It was slow at first, but then she was loudly sobbing.

Thoughts of the hope of a future; thoughts of what could be and could've been; memories of all the times that were past, and dreams of all the futures that could come true, all flashed through Elliana's mind as she cried and mourned the loss of her neighbors, her friends, their families, Vell, Ms. Keiara, Mr. Tilian, and so on and so on.

So many lives, so many stories, so many futures... extinguished, she thought.

The girls had lost themselves in their grief and their sorrow. At one point, Mira had gotten up and started screaming and banging and hitting and throwing things. She yelled words of hatred, words of grief, words that beg for forgiveness, until words no longer could describe what she wanted to say or what she was feeling. Her friends were gone, her cousin that had followed her to this town was gone, almost everyone she knew in this town were either gone or suffering because their family was gone, even if they did not know it yet.

The day wore on as the girls became lethargic and sat there. No one came to visit them, and even if they did, the girls would not have been in the right state of mind to process the audio cue of a knock on the door.

Eventually, Tatiana started to mill about, first pacing and then practicing her forms. Mira alternated between outbursts and then laying on the floor or against the wall in depression. Elliana, well Elliana realized that she had fallen asleep and hoped that she had not snored. Eventually she got up as well and started fighting an imaginary opponent. Soon, it was a real opponent as Mira silently joined her, then Tatiana joined in, and before they knew it, they were in the midst of a never-ending spar battle between Mira, Tatiana and Elliana.

Over the course of the next few days, that is what they did: mindlessly fighting each other (with the occasional corrections from Mira), each silently evolving in their form of combat. They used routine as a crutch against their sadness and depression: they came to the guild, ate, practiced, ate, practiced, and then ate, and then, maybe, went home late.

Over the same period, the news spread throughout the town. People were affected, businesses were affected, life was affected – nothing was the same.

Then the sadness and loss rippled into other events. People stopped working or doing anything; people moved; people disappeared; people sold their processions so they could move or pay off debts they had incurred now that the family's breadwinner were dead or missing; and so on and so on.

Tatiana could be a brat, she knew, but she did not want to burden the family. Their main breadwinner was gone now, so her brothers had to stop being immature and do something to bring in money. They weren't going to become mercenaries like they had wanted to. Mr. Tilian was right in not letting them become mercenaries. He saw that they did not have the desire or the desperation for it. The family had gathered some property that they were going to take care of. They also helped a friend by taking over his store so they could go to Fort Holden to help people and search for his missing son.

Tatiana's mother was in grief. She had always been strong, even with Mr. Tilian. But she could barely do her own housework now. Their youngest, a daughter, helped her mother with everything. School had been suspended, so it was okay for her to be at home.

It was good that Elliana, Tatiana, and Lucinda had graduated a few weeks prior to receiving the news. It was a happy time, a joyous time, filled with celebration and hope for a future. Now, many of the students and former students of the school, as well as the teachers and staff, had lost someone. Whether a family member or a friend, they all had lost someone.

Lucinda's family took almost everything they had to the fort to help the survivors. It was big business to their family, but it was still difficult for them to separate the fact that they were treating friends and families. They left one of their younger daughters, Luda, to mind the store while they were gone. She could not diagnose patients, but she could still sell basic medicines and remedies. And most of the town simply needed medicine for pain relief or pain relief for the other type of pain.

Elliana's family had always helped to take care of people's property while they were away or if they weren't able to. So it was natural for the people to continue to depend on Elliana's family, more so than usual. However, the changes to the town caused some of the help to be more desperate than they used to be. And different people came to Elliana's family for help. Most could no longer afford to keep their properties, their homes, their lands, and even their belongings. A lot of people were desperate to sell things so they could pay off debts or because they needed to move.

Elliana had always felt that her family was modest, maybe even below modest. She had seen the fancier and more expensive houses in town, or the opulence of some of the people. Even the modest house that Vell and Keiara lived in seemed to be more inviting than her own home. She did love her home and her family, but she had always felt disadvantaged when she compared herself to other people. So Elliana could not help but be surprised to learn how close some of these people were to the edge of ruin. And of course, it was surprising that these people would be so desperate that they had to turn to her family.

It got to the point where people were practically begging her family to buy their stuff. Some of them even went as far as trading grand decorations and ornate fixtures for more practical things like food or a wagon for transportation. And Elliana's father and mother both helped as much as they could, willing to stockpile things that used to make Elliana sick with envy but now she was just sick of their sight. She had been so used to her simple life that now that her house was full of things she felt frustrated.

She could not hold it in any longer.

"Dad," she said one night as her parents continued their ritual of asking if she was okay, "why are we collecting all this stuff – all this junk, other people's junk?"

"That's a good question, dear," her father said. "It's just that with all that has happened, people need help."

"And how does it help them? Or us!?" Elliana said.

Her father and mother looked at each other, not sure what to say.

"Sometimes, when people spend too much, they might not have enough for emergencies," she said, trying to explain. "So now they need help selling whatever they can, doing whatever they can, because of the emergencies."

Elliana pouted. Maybe she wanted to be selfish for the moment. Maybe she was sad that people were so quick to abandon her hometown. Maybe it was because she was just frustrated by all the stuff, maybe just frustrated with everything. She wished that, for once, her family thought of themselves... their future. How does buying all these useless things help when her family had an emergency of their own?

And she asked that question to her parents.

They both just smiled.

"We're okay," her father said as he returned to poking his food. "We're not spending more than we have."

"But some of these things are not cheap!" Elliana had seen the prices of some of the items in her house, and they made her jaw drop. Now, somehow, it was in her home.

"Well, we don't buy them at full price, Elliana," her mother said. "People who are desperate to sell will sell things cheaply. And we bargain too, because we can't afford to help everyone if they sell them at full price. Most people need to get rid of the stuff so they can leave or pay off their debts."

"Yeah," Elliana's father said. "And when people suddenly want the same things, the price for it goes up. Like caravan wagons. After the supplies were delivered to Fort Holden when the mission first started, no one wanted them. They were basically giving them away once they returned to town. Now, people are giving up almost everything to get even a bit of space on one of those wagons."

Her father suddenly looked up at her mother, as if he said something he was not supposed to. Elliana's mother smiled though, as if she were holding back a laugh.

"Go ahead, tell her," she said.

A grin appeared on her father's face.

"So, you know the warehouses by the river, next to the mill?" Elliana's father said. Elliana nodded slowly. She was wary of the secret her parents were about to tell her. "Well, we own it now."

"What?! How?" she yelled, incredulous. It was so unbelievable that she had jumped out of her seat.

Her parents laughed.

"The owners, Mr. Skorzky and his family, had to leave but they also had a lot of debt for the goods and the warehouses. So I negotiated with him to take on their debt in exchange for the warehouses and stuff inside."

"Let's just say that he needed quite a few wagons and quite a few other things that he had not prepared for," Elliana's mother added with a chuckle.

"But that means we are in debt!" Elliana cried.

"Well, not all debt is bad," her father started to say, but then he waved his hands in the air like a nervous magician. "No, no, that doesn't matter, because we don't have debt."

Before she could ask, Elliana's mother answered. "We traded the wagons and provisions, plus the agreement to the debt and even their obligations here as part of their company," she said.

"Yeah, complicated stuff..." her father interrupted while wiping his mouth with a napkin.

"And we, in turn, negotiated with the other people to lower or get rid of their debt and obligations in exchange for other things," she continued. "So, long story short, we don't have debt, but we do have warehouses of perishable goods that will need to be sold or exchanged quickly."

Perishable goods? Obligations? Company agreements? It all made Elliana's head spin. She had no idea how her parents had even learnt of the terms, let alone learned how to work with and around them.

"Your mother is a miracle worker," Elliana's father said, interrupting her thoughts. "A lot of those tedious negations were handled by her, even the ones with the bank."

"Oh, it was nothing," her mother said with a cheeky smile and a wave of her hand.

It obviously was not nothing. In fact, it sounded very complicated.

"So, yeah, we now own a mansion that is as big as a warehouse," her father said.

"You mean, a warehouse that is as big as a mansion?" Elliana said, questioning the question.

"Oops, yeah, that's what I meant," her father said with a wink to her mother. Elliana's mother did not return the wink. She just sat with her cup to her lips that still formed a knowing smile.

It took a long moment before Elliana realized what had just been said. Understandably, she started choking on her food. It was easily cleared through an ugly fit of coughing.

"How did you even know how to do all this?" Elliana gasped the question as the coughing fit had strained her throat. "It's all so complicated."

"Well, the bank did not want people to suddenly take out all their money, because…" her mother started to say.

"No, no," Elliana coughed again. "I mean, yes, but how did you figure out how to do all this?"

Her father cleared his throat dramatically and answered with a smile. "Over the years, Ms. Ke.." and then he stopped suddenly, smile disappearing just as quickly. It took a moment before he could continue again. "... Ms. Keiara had helped us a long time ago, and she also explained to us how things worked. In fact, she had advised against buying too much land because she had seen how land became worthless when the Scourge were on it. But, you know..." his words cracked in his throat.

"All those 'adult talks', we had over the years," Elliana's mother added softly. Her eyes looked moist.

Elliana felt sad again. It was funny that for a brief moment, thoughts of worry had been a good break from the sadness that ached her heart and caused the rest of her body to remain numb.

"Once upon a time, the adult talk was also adult talk to us," her father said, breaking the silence. "Until we realized that it applied to our lives and affected us, whether we knew it or not. Anyways..."

The silence continued.

"I had been prepared for Ms. Keiara to... you know," Elliana's mother said, the tears dripping into her cup. "Or at least, I thought I had. But Vell..."

Hearing the name in the air had made Elliana want to cry again.

"He's such a good lad, an odd one, but a good one," her father said.

"Shush," her mother said. "They could still be alive."

Elliana's father nodded.

"I had always thought of the different ways we could help Vell," Elliana's mother continued, despite telling her husband to shush. "We could adopt him, or be his guardians, or maybe he could marry Elliana and be our son-in-law."

"What?" Elliana reflexively said.

"I-It was just a thought," her mother said, blushing, "I mean, he is a handsome boy, and you're close to him."

"Besides can you imagine him with... I don't know... Lucinda? Or even Tatiana?" Elliana's father added.

The thought of Tatiana and Vell married, let alone to each other, made Elliana laugh.

She laughed so hard that she cried.

And her parents joined her.

"Oh, Vell..." Elliana's mother said, shaking her head and wiping her eyes.

Life continued as usual in the town, which is to say that it continued to be terrible.

The decline continued as people were faced with desperation. Townsfolk who could help, helped – like her parents did. It was always a difficult affair for both sides and it was painful to watch.

To shield herself from the events and to distract her mind from the sadness, Elliana continued to spend her days at the guild in training. She did not really know if she wanted to be a mercenary, but she continued to train anyway as a sort of therapy. Maybe one day, even if she were not a mercenary, she would find her training useful. In any case, training was a much better use of her time than moping around.

"Rider! We've got a rider here!"

Since the catastrophe at the Wall, news had slowly trickled in. Normally, towns like this one would have been the last to know, but since so many of the people from this town were involved, news came in more often through messengers on horseback. Everyone referred to these messengers as riders.

At first, Elliana, Tatiana and Mira would rush out to hear the news. However, the news was hardly ever good. It was mostly news about confirmation of the dead, or how someone was seriously injured and will be in recovery. Apparently the chaos of the whole thing had made it difficult to figure out who had died, who had survived or who was still unaccounted for.

Eventually, the girls just ignored the calls as the riders came in to the guild and, after some time, began to be annoyed by it.

"Are you...?" Tatiana asked Elliana as she swung her sword and clashed with Elliana's.

"Nope, not even," Elliana responded in words as well as with her sword.

Mira just leaned her back against the wall of the training room as she recovered from an intense routine. It was late, almost time for dinner, but no one seemed to want to go home. Elliana knew that she should go see her parents, but her body continued to match Tatiana's light sparring.

After a long while, Mira slowly stood up, drained her water container, and said, "Well, I better go check the news, and help the guildmaster deal with people's grief... again."

Elliana and Tatiana did not envy Mira.

Since the guildmaster had fainted, Mira had somehow stepped in to help with his responsibilities. Sure, there were older guild members still around, and there were even active guild members with more experience than Mira, but none of them fit the bill for whatever reason.

"It's just temporary," Mira had said when asked about it.

But it was starting to feel like the guildmaster was slowly passing things on to her. The weight of the decision to go through with the mission as well as the toll of dealing with the aftermath must be difficult for the guildmaster to bear.

Mira didn't come back that evening after she left.

"It must've been bad," Tatiana said as she and Elliana trudged home.

"Worse than usual?" Elliana said.

Tatiana just laughed.

It hurt Elliana to see her friend like this. To an outsider, it was the same old Tatiana. However, Elliana knew she had changed. Tatiana was still holding onto the hope that her father had survived and forgotten to tell them again. But no news had come in from him... or about him.

After seeing Tatiana home, Elliana walked to the edge of town where she still stayed with her parents. As tempting as it was to move to one of the various properties that her family now owned, it did not seem like it would be wise to. It might appear to others that her family was taking advantage of people's plight. It was sort of true, but it was done in the spirit of helping people through the tragedy. Besides, she liked her home. It was... home.

As she approached her house, she saw lights on in Ms. Keiara and Vell's house.

That's strange, she thought.

She was sure she had not left anything on that would show a light. All fires were out, all lanterns were extinguished – nothing should be putting out light. She wondered if it was her mother that had done something in the house. It was a little odd, but then again, Elliana had come back late.

She silenced her steps and diminished her presence as she carefully approached the house. The curtains had been drawn close and prevented her from seeing into the house. She wondered if her mother had done that, because she left the curtains wide open when she went to the guild.

Elliana went through the possible scenarios in her head. If it was just her mother, it would not be a problem. If Elliana had just left something lit, then that might be a small problem and she did not want her parents to know. However, if someone else was inside the house, then that would be bad.

But who would be in the house? Her mother? Her father? Vell?

At the thought of Vell being in the house, Elliana found herself opening the door. She had dropped her bag, but still carried a metal training sword.

So when she opened the door and found a strange man in the house, she was able to quickly draw her training sword and defend herself against the man.

"W-Who are you!?" she yelled at the man, who had turned to look at Elliana in surprise. His back was facing the door, so Elliana had the upper hand. But the man had armor on – not heavy armor, but it was more armor than what Elliana was wearing.

The man did not answer her. Elliana did not recognize the man at all.

"Who are you!?" she screamed, much louder this time. "Why are you in this house?"

"C-Calm down, girl," the man said. He had put the spoon in his hand down, and calmly tried to get up. But before he could lift himself up out of the seat, Elliana made a threatening motion with her sword. The man promptly sat back down.

Now that Elliana had the man stuck in his chair, she wondered what would be the next move. She was at the edge of town and she was not even sure her parents were in. The closest neighbors may not have been in their houses either – so many of them had moved in recent days.

Now what!? Elliana screamed silently to herself.

And another disturbing thought crossed her mind: what if this man was not alone? Maybe that's why he looked so relax as he ate his soup.

A creaking sound to the right of her sent chills down her spine and into the sword. Her fears had been realized. There was someone else and now he was coming down the stairs.

The man glanced towards the stairs, and it confirmed it.

What do I do!? What do I do!? she thought.

Her heart beat faster and faster. She felt that her face clearly betrayed her nervousness. It was getting harder and harder for her to breathe properly.

Should I run? Should I face the second person? Should run the man through?

She was surprised at her own thoughts. Apparently the scenarios that she used to liven up her training had materialized in the real world, and there was no room for error.

The man seemed relax.

"May I continue to eat my dinner?" the man asked Elliana.

"Y-Yes," she stammered, the request throwing her off. "B-But both hands on the table where I can see them." The man calmly and deliberately complied. Then he continued eating his soup.

After a tense moment of waiting, Elliana called out to her parents, but she did not hear a response. She called again. The same response. She did not risk it again.

"W-Who are you?" she asked again as she turned her attention to the man. But then she heard a creak and turned to face it out of reflexes. However, that left her facing the opposite direction of the man.

She silently chided herself and braced for the next movement.

A voice came from the stairs. "That is Captain Wilhelm," the voice said. "He saved my life and now he has taken me home, as he has promised."

The figure came down the final steps of the staircase and the light revealed his features clearly. It was Vell. He had just had a bath and was toweling his hair dry.

Elliana could not help but drop her sword and run to hug Vell.

"You're alive!" she yelled into his neck. Then she realized what she had done and suddenly let go of Vell. In that moment, she looked at Vell's face – closer than she's seen before – and saw a smile on his face.

"Yes, I'm alive," he said before the smile faded away.

Just then, Elliana's parents burst through the open doorway, with a neighbor in tow. They spotted the man, and in their panic, they saw their daughter next to another strange person.

"Get away from her!" Elliana's mother said as she rushed to Vell with some sort of wooden weapon in her hand.

"Mom!" Elliana yelled, blocking Vell. "It's Vell. He's back."

Her mother paused for a bit, but seemed unconvinced. Elliana then grabbed Vell, just the side of his tunic, and pulled him closer to the light.

"Oh, it's Vell!" Elliana's mother exclaimed as she dropped the weapon in her hand and moved towards Vell. Elliana looked down at the weapon, and was surprised to see it was a spiked club, a bloody sort of weapon. Elliana pretended not to see it and waved away the mental questions she had about it and how it ended up in her gentle mother's hand.

After exchanging pleasantries, things settled down though the man and Vell looked exhausted.

"We had stopped by the guild to give a quick update, but Vell wanted to leave as soon as he could," the man, Captain Wilhelm, said.

"Weren't you at the guild as well, Elliana?" her mother asked.

"Yes, but we didn't really want to hear anymore news about people deaths," Elliana answered dryly. Apparently the riders that had come in earlier were Vell and the Captain.

"So, what's the word? What about your mother?" Elliana's mother asked.

The Captain shifted uncomfortably in his chair. Vell remained quiet.

Elliana had a bad feeling. She felt tears starting to well up in her eyes. She looked down in an effort to hide them, and for the tears to quickly fall out of sight.

"Don't know," Vell finally answered, his voice barely above a whisper.

An awkward silence filled the room.

"W-What about Mr. Tilian?" Elliana bravely asked. She did not want to know, but she knew that her friend would want to know.

Vell shook his head slowly. Then he looked down at the ground.

Elliana's mother gasped softly as she brought her hand to her lips. Elliana knew that the optimism and happiness that her mother had shown was just a performance, maybe at times it was also a sign of hope, but either way her face darkened as she realized the gravity of the two missing people.

The silence settled in again, and it threatened to smother them this time.

But Elliana's mother suddenly sprang up, as if she had just eaten sunshine and bouncy springs.

"I-It's okay, Vell," she said, holding her fist tightly in the air, "you can be our son, we'll adopt you. Or better yet, you can marry Elliana and it'll solve another of our worries. Or..."

"Mom!" Elliana yelled, partially out of anger but mostly out of embarrassment.

Captain Wilhelm chuckled. "You've got that going for you, Vell, a nice home, a nice family, and a pretty wife," he said to Vell.

Vell chuckled softly as well, which surprised Elliana. "But how can she be married to Death?" he said.

"Come on, Vell, you're not still..." the Captain stood up and said loudly.

Vell snapped back. "Of course I am! There is no way I'm going to..." Vell noticed the two ladies in his presence and stopped yelling. "Never mind," he said softly before sitting back down.

Elliana did not know what to think of that outburst. She looked at her mother, and her mother looked at her. Then she looked at the both the Captain and Vell. They both looked like they had been over this before.

A question suddenly popped into Elliana's mind. She knew she had to ask no matter what.

"Vell..?" she said meekly. Vell looked up at her. She walked closer to Vell, softly, gently.

"Are you going to propose to him?" Elliana's mother interrupted. It was like a lightning bolt through Elliana's back.

"Mom!"

"Sorry, but are you?" she asked, pushing the joke too far.

The Captain laughed.

"Well, I was going to ask Vell about…someone," she said. After a brief moment to steel herself, she finally asked. "Do you know what happened to Bernard?"

Vell's expression changed to a quizzical one.

"Bernard?" the Captain said. "That Bernard?"

Elliana had no idea which Bernard he was referring to.

"Mira's cousin, Bernard," she said.

Vell sat up straight. "Bernard? He's fine. He's still at the Fort. One of the few that was able enough to stay on the line, and willing enough to take the contract."

"That Bernard?" the Captain said again. Vell nodded to him. "Looks like you have some competition, Vell," the Captain responded.

Elliana blushed. "N-No, it's just that I've been training with Mira," she said.

"Oh, yes, Mira mentioned that," Vell said.

"Oh, so she knows?" she asked. Vell nodded his head.

"That Bernard is something else," the Captain said. "He woke up and dragged people out of harm's way. Then he kept going back even though the enemy could attack at any time. All that with broken ribs."

"Cracked ribs," Vell said.

"They hurt just the same, Vell," the Captain retorted.

As the night faded on, someone decided it was time to sleep. Vell's house only had two rooms and he did not want anyone sleeping on his mother's bed. The Captain was offered a number of other alternatives, such as a nice room at the inn, or a place at Elliana's house, but he decided to sleep near the fire on the ground floor of Vell's house. Vell wanted him to sleep in nicer accommodations, but the Captain assured him that this was better than what he was used to.

So Elliana and her mother bid good night and went back to their home to finish up and go to sleep.

But sleep did not stay very long with Elliana.

She woke to the sound of arguing outside her house. Being this far on the outskirts of town meant that it was strange on multiple levels.

She crept into the main living area and found that the argument had woken her parents as well.

"What's going on?" Elliana asked.

"Vell and the Captain are arguing," Elliana's mother said.

Elliana went to the window to take a look for herself.

"Vell, please settle down," the Captain implored. Vell had just walked into the house. "I'll help you, or if you don't want my help, at least let the neighbors help you."

Vell came back out, carrying something. He dumped it next to the horses that had been tied outside. "I thought I could, Captain, but I can't.... I can't sleep in that house. Everything reminds me of her and her absence. And remembering her reminds me of the people in power who let this happen."

"They're not going to open the Wall again, not just for you," the Captain continued. "And you cannot just go and kill people like you did on the battlefield. It'll be murder. You'll lose everything."

"I don't care!" Vell said as he went back into the house again.

"Well, you should!" the Captain screamed at him, no longer able to control his rage any longer. "You have a nice home, people that care for you and that want to take care of you, and you are a talented young person – a whole future is in front of you."

Vell came out again. "But that won't bring back my mother."

"Neither is getting yourself killed fighting the Scourge, or getting yourself thrown into prison for killing the elites."

Vell stopped in his tracks. His eyes, downcast. "I know, Captain," Vell said, his voice cracking. "But what am I supposed to do with all this rage? This anger? This grief?" He choked on his spit and started coughing. You could hear him starting to cry. "Nothing matters anymore," he said. "I need to do something. And I know I can't sleep in that house tonight, and I won't be able to sleep in there tomorrow night, or the next night...maybe in the future, but not if I keep trying to sleep here."

Elliana couldn't help herself. She rushed out of the house and ran to Vell.

"Vell, you're not leaving, are you?" she asked.

Vell paused. It seemed that the third voice was completely unexpected.

"I..." Vell started to say. His back continued to be turned to Elliana and he made no moves to look at her.

"Vell?"

Elliana shivered in the cold breeze of the early morning. The warms tears that rolled down her cheeks were the only source of heat, of comfort, as the breeze picked up. She wrapped her arms around herself, realizing how vulnerable she was in her light clothing. But she did not want to move, or even flinch, for fear that it would be the last time she ever saw Vell.

"Yes," Vell finally said. For a moment, Elliana had forgotten the question. By the time she remembered, Vell had walked back into his house, his eyes never looked away from the ground.

A soft sob escaped Elliana's lips. She did not know what to do. She looked at Captain Wilhelm who had slumped onto a bench outside. He looked defeated as well. Elliana turned to look at her house, hoping her parents would come out to help

– at least with a coat – but they continued to watch from the window, maybe hoping it was a rare romantic moment that Elliana and Vell could take advantage of.

Vell came out of the house again, with something in his hands. It was a small satchel, but it looked heavy. With it, there were a few odd items. Vell, reluctant to look up from the ground, walked up to Elliana and put the items gently into her hands.

"For you," he said softly. He glanced upward for a second with a guilty look in his eyes, and then quickly looked back down like looking at Elliana was crime.

Elliana blinked away the tears and steadied her voice. "What is it?"

"It's some money," he said, "and a bank book."

Elliana clumsily opened the satchel in surprise. She saw the coins and other forms of currency in the bag. It was more than she had ever seen in her life. She refused to accept it. It was too much.

Besides, she would trade all that in an instant to have Vell stay.

Vell shook his head. "No, it's for you. Please look after our house... my mother and my ... mine... whatever... the house," he stumbled over his words. Usually he would sit quietly and only spoke occasionally, with perfect sentences or short replies. It was strange for him to stumble so much. "I-I also opened a bank account for you," he continued. Elliana's eyes widen in shock. She could not believe she had a bank account. But how could he open an account without her? "It already has some money in it. I was going to put this in tomorrow before I left... I wanted to say a proper goodbye to everyone, but I can't... I can't stand it anymore... I have to leave."

"H-How did you open an account for me, and why?" Elliana asked. She couldn't bring herself to ask why he was leaving. She wanted to deny that as long as she could – stall him, even.

He looked at her and smiled, forgetting the forbidden-ness of the act from earlier. "Do you remember the time we went to the bank and filled out the form? The one you didn't submit?" Elliana nodded. It was such a beautiful day. "Well, I turned it in and put in money for you. I was going to give it to you after... after... after we came home from the mission. I wanted to give you some of the reward money so you could buy something or use it or save it...I don't know... but..." he remembered himself and looked down at the ground again. "I guess shit happens."

Elliana was surprised at the use of the word. It was never used around town, and never by Vell. Sure, she knew about it and even heard it occasionally in the guild, but it was always something that crass people said. Not Vell.

But a pang in her heart told her that she already knew it but did not want to admit it – that she knew Vell had changed.

Elliana took a deep breath and sucked in the melancholy that was about to ooze out again.

"Anyways, please take care of the house for me... I'll deposit money into your account occasionally, but please take care of the house for me... my h-house," Vell said. His voice started to crack under the strain of his emotions. Elliana saw how hard Vell tried to suppress his emotions. "Maybe, one day, I'll be able to come back... but for now, I can't... the memories, the smells, the sight... I can't... and I cannot taint this house with my anger... not this perfect place." Vell gasped as a surprise sob tried to escape his lips, but he held it back while sucking in the air. He trembled as he stood there.

Then he turned around and walked away. Both of his arms were at his side balled into tight fists. The march into his house was awkward and halting.

But he stopped just before he entered and turned back to Elliana. Before she understood what was going on, Vell had embraced her, deeply, and held on so tight that it hurt. But it was a good hurt. The warmth spread through her body as she felt the cold surface of his armor against her skin, and felt the warmth fight off the cold. His head rested on her shoulder and his face was in the crook of her neck, just between the nape and her shoulder. It was such a personal embrace, almost a lovers' embrace. But Elliana did not have time to think of those abstract thoughts, she just thought of the present feeling that enveloped her.

"I'm sorry," Vell said before he finally let go and went back into the house.

Elliana just stood there – the tears flew freely down her cheeks but did not obstruct her view. The warmth still enveloped her. It also seemed to root her to that spot and refused to let her move as Vell continued to pack his things. Elliana's parents had finally come out of their house. They made their own attempts to get Vell to stay.

But to no avail.

Finally, Vell was ready. The light had risen just enough to give the dark skies a little bit of glow. He bid farewell, even briefly hugging Elliana's parents. Captain Wilhelm was stubborn: he did not want to hug Vell. However, he finally relented in a firm handshake after Vell assured him that Captain Wilhelm had fulfilled his promise to his mother, even if the Captain did not feel like he had.

Then Vell approached Elliana. Dazed and overwhelmed, she had not moved from the spot; her body had refused to let her move. Vell looked like a child who had done something wrong and was timidly approaching to apologize.

"V-Vell..." Elliana finally said as she looked at him.

Vell looked up and looked straight into her eyes. The moment seemed to last forever, but then Vell hugged Elliana deeply again.

"Sorry," he said. Then he held onto Elliana for a long time.

Finally, before he let go, he whispered softly into her ears, "Be happy."

And then he let go.

Forever.

MANSFRED SWRIT